Phyllis Reynolds Naylor
and Lura Schield Reynolds

MAUDIE
in the
MIDDLE

Illustrated by Judith Gwyn Brown

A JEAN KARL BOOK

Atheneum · 1988 · New York

Text copyright © 1988 by Phyllis Reynolds Naylor
and Lura Schield Reynolds
Illustrations copyright © 1988 by Judith Gwyn Brown

Atheneum
Macmillan Publishing Company
866 Third Avenue, New York, NY 10022
Collier Macmillan Canada, Inc.

Type set by Arcata Graphics/Kingsport, Kingsport, Tennessee
Printed and bound by Fairfield Graphics, Fairfield, Pennsylvania
Designed by Mary Ahern
First Edition

10   9   8   7   6   5   4   3   2   1

Library of Congress Cataloging-in-Publication Data

Naylor, Phyllis Reynolds.   Maudie in the middle.

SUMMARY: Maudie, one of a large family growing up in Iowa
in the early 1900s, seems to attract nothing but
trouble when all she wants is to be noticed for herself;
and when a crisis hits the family she finally accomplishes this
in the best way possible.
[1. Family life—Fiction.   2. Iowa—Fiction]
I. Reynolds, Lura Schield.   II. Brown, Judith Gwyn, ill.
III. Title.
PZ7.N24.Mau   1988   [Fic]   87–3470
ISBN 0-689-31395-0

This story is based, in part, on my mother's written account of her life in Sioux County, Iowa, in the early 1900s. And so we dedicate it, she and I, to the memory of her parents, Fred and Emma Schield, and her older brother, Ray, and to her five surviving brothers and sisters: Myrtle, Vern, Russell, Wilbur, & Viola.

—Phyllis Reynolds Naylor

Contents

MAUDIE
in the
MIDDLE

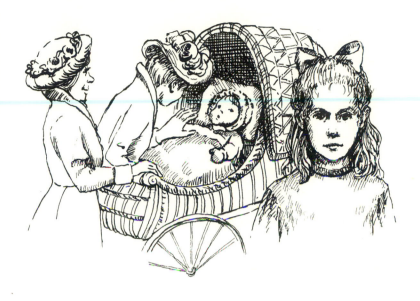

1

The Potato Baby

Mrs. Franklin's baby slobbered. He sucked noisily on one fist, and didn't even know that the two women had been talking about him—only him and nobody else—for five minutes. Maudie gave small impatient tugs at her mother's arm.

"Such a *healthy* baby," Maudie's mother said, bending over the carriage again and cooing, her lips in the shape of an O.

He's fat! Maudie wanted to say. All this fuss about a fat baby who made disgusting noises.

"You should see the way he eats potato," Mrs. Franklin went on, and Maudie had to listen to a list of all the foods the fat baby loved to eat. She had already heard about the number of times he belched after every feeding, as if anyone cared.

Maudie wanted to go down the street to Black's Dry-Goods Store, where she could buy a little wooden monkey suspended between two sticks. When you squeezed the sticks together, the monkey did somersaults. She tugged again at her mother's arm.

"Of course, the potato has to be mashed just right," Mrs. Franklin was saying. "Not a single lump, or it comes back up."

Maudie felt a belch of her own coming on. Yes, she was sure of it. Just a tiny little bubble of gas, but it seemed to grow larger the higher it got in her throat, and when it reached her mouth, she didn't close her lips as her mother had taught her to do, but let it come right out. *Burp!*

"Maudie *Mae!*" said her mother. "Where are your manners?"

It seemed to Maudie that there were lots of things you could get away with if you were young enough, and quite a few others that you could do if you were older. Maudie, however, was caught in the middle. Three of the Simmses' children were older than she and three were younger, and the only thing special about Maudie herself was that she had been born in the year 1900.

"My turn-of-the-century child," Father called her sometimes.

Now Maudie's mother and Mrs. Franklin were talking about clothes—about nightshirts and woolen booties and embroidered gowns and caps. Maudie leaned over the carriage herself, her back to the women, and made her most terrible face, pushing her nose up with two fingers and pulling down the skin beneath her eyes. The baby studied her intently and blew bubbles from his lips.

Babies always got the best of things, Maudie was thinking. Sammy and Violet, the two youngest children in her own family, got the choice bites of food at the table, just because they were little. And all Mrs. Franklin's baby had to do was lie in his carriage and grunt, and his mother thought he was wonderful. Maudie almost had to stand on her head to get her mother to notice her, and she could not remember one single time in her whole life that Mama had said she was wonderful or that she had missed her or that she loved her so very, very much.

Across the street, a young boy was holding a long

The Potato Baby

stick with a toy bird on the end. When he swung the stick around, the bird made a whistling sound. Maudie thought of Black's store again, and wondered if perhaps she might like a toy bird instead of a monkey.

"Mama," she whispered, tugging at her mother's hand, but Mother paid no attention. Maudie stretched her mother's arm out straight and practiced turning around beneath it, as though they were dancing there on the sidewalk. Faster and faster she whirled, holding her mother's hand, until Mother herself was moving from side to side as she carried on the conversation with Mrs. Franklin.

"Stop that!" Mother said suddenly, and rapped Maudie sharply on the shoulder.

Mrs. Franklin was looking at Maudie disapprovingly. Maudie ducked behind her mother and stood with her eyes down, hidden by her mother's long wool coat. How embarrassed she was.

It was always like this. The few times that Maudie had Mother to herself, some*thing* or some*one* got in the way. The more Maudie wanted to be noticed for being wonderful, the more attention she got for being bad.

If this had been Aunt Sylvie instead of Mother, she would have smiled at Maudie dancing on the sidewalk. She might even have laughed and taken

Maudie in the Middle

a whirl or two herself. She would have known, without Maudie having to tell her, that Maudie was eager to get to Black's store. And once there, she would have stopped to wind up the toys herself, holding up the dolls to see what they were wearing underneath, and giving Maudie all the time in the world to decide what it was she wanted to buy. With Mother, there were just too many children to look after, too much to do, too little time.

Maudie had a wish, a secret wish, that some day she would be Aunt Sylvie's godchild. She was not even sure what a godchild was—somebody very good, she decided. Anne Hubbell, at school, was the godchild of Mrs. Hubbell's best friend, and she said that this friend took her to special places, bought her special things, and that if anything ever happened to her own mother, this friend was to take care of Anne and love her always.

Aunt Sylvie was Mother's younger sister and her best friend—the perfect one to be Maudie's godmother. If Aunt Sylvie had wanted to choose Claire, Maudie's older sister, for a godchild, she would have done it by now, and Violet was still a baby. Maudie couldn't imagine anyone choosing a *boy* to be a godchild. So whenever Maudie was around her Aunt Sylvie she tried to be perfect, in the hope that some day, when she was ten, perhaps, Aunt Sylvie would

The Potato Baby

announce to the family that Maudie was to be her godchild.

Right now, however, standing there behind Mother on the brick sidewalk with Aunt Sylvie nowhere in sight, Maudie felt angry at all her brothers and sisters who used up Mama's time. She was especially furious at Mrs. Franklin's fat baby, who was getting all the attention. A surrey clattered by on the street with the Wheelers in it, and both Mother and Mrs. Franklin turned to wave. In that moment Maudie reached over, gave the fat baby a hard pinch on the arm, and slipped back behind her mother so fast that when the baby howled, neither of the women guessed what had happened.

"Ohhhh!" Maudie said tenderly, leaning over the edge of the carriage. "What's the matter, little baby?"

"Waaah!" the potato baby wailed, legs kicking.

"Gas," said Mrs. Franklin. "He gets a bubble, he lets you know."

Maudie gently patted the baby's head and rocked the carriage back and forth.

"Maudie just loves babies," said her mother.

Maudie tried not to look at the baby, tried not to listen as his crying turned to indignant little whines, tried not to feel the way her ears burned. It was the nicest thing her mother had said about her for months and months and months, and it

Maudie in the Middle

wasn't even true. She continued rocking the carriage, and when Mother was ready to leave at last, the baby was holding on to one of Maudie's fingers.

Maudie clung tightly to her mother's arm as they went on down the sidewalk. Maybe she could still be that special daughter she wanted so desperately to be. It was a rare occasion when Maudie got to come into town on Saturdays. Her father and two older brothers would be waiting for them at the feed store, but for right now it was just Maudie Mae and her mother together.

"What did *I* like to eat when *I* was a little baby, Mama?" she asked.

Mrs. Simms sighed. "I don't know, Maudie. There are so many of you, I can never keep you straight. Seems to me you might have liked potato too, but it's just not the sort of thing I'd remember."

2

Uncle Wilfred's Ear

In winter, Maudie's house was full of people. On a cold March Sunday after church, in fact, the house hardly seemed big enough for all the people in it.

To begin with, there were all the Simmses' children, who, if you arranged them like stair steps, were Joe, 17, the oldest; Claire, who was 14; Vernon, 11; Maudie Mae, 8 years old; Lester, 7; Sammy, 5; and little Violet, who was still a baby. Then there was Aunt Sylvie, who lived with the family, and anybody else who Maudie's father might have invited home to dinner after church.

"Brother Bliss might be by for dinner," Father said, as he hung up his Sunday hat. The family always spoke of their minister as *Brother,* and his wife was known as *Sister* Bliss.

Mother and Aunt Sylvie exchanged exasperated glances.

"Well, what did he say, Tom? Yes or no?" Mother asked.

Father thought it over. "Think he said yes, but then he said something about asking the wife. . . ."

"Maybe they already had an invitation somewhere else," Aunt Sylvie suggested.

Mother sighed as she tied an apron over her taffeta dress. "Maudie . . . ," she said, and Maudie promptly took her place at the parlor window overlooking the front lawn. It was her job on Sundays to watch for the company her father had invited, because no one was ever quite sure they would come.

"Sister Bliss has her grown nephew staying the month," Aunt Sylvie reminded. "He'll eat up all the pie and then some."

"That's *three* extra plates, then," Mother said from the kitchen. "I *wish* Tom would get it straight. It's not that I mind. . . ."

Maudie pulled her legs up under her on the big

chair by the parlor window and played with her toy monkey as she watched for the minister's buggy. Little Violet had been placed in the center of the floor on the carpet, surrounded by cushions to keep her in, and Maudie was supposed to watch her, too, while Mother, Aunt Sylvie, and Claire made dinner.

It was always an occasion when the Blisses came to dinner. Maudie could never understand how, after preaching such a long sermon in church, the minister could find enough words left to pray a long prayer at the Simmses' table. But no matter how long it went on, even if the gravy was getting cold, Sister Bliss just sat with the most blessed smile on her face. Maudie could never stop staring.

Some company paid no attention to children at all, and it was as though Maudie and her brothers and sisters weren't even there. The minister and his wife, however, always took time to say something special to each child, and Maudie wondered what they would notice about her today. Perhaps Sister Bliss would tell Mother how Maudie had memorized her Bible verse perfectly that morning. Or she would admire the extra large ribbon that Maudie wore in her hair. Perhaps Brother Bliss would compliment her on sitting so quietly through his sermon, not even getting up once to go to the outhouse.

The boys kept on their good clothes in case the

minister and his wife came to dinner. Vernon, Lester, and Sammy all wore knee pants, but Joe wore long trousers like Father. All of Maudie's brothers sat together now in the sitting room off the kitchen, looking at pictures through the stereoscope.

To Maudie, the stereoscope looked like a huge pair of eyeglasses, with a holder sticking out in front where you slipped each postcard-size picture, one at a time. When you looked at a card without the stereoscope, it looked like two pictures of the same thing, side by side. But when you looked at the card through the stereoscope, it appeared to be only one picture, so real you felt you were right there in it. The Simmses had a collection of stereoscopic pictures of Yellowstone Park and the Spanish-American War, and Joe had just bought a dozen comic views for 56¢. The boys were urging each other to hurry so that each one could use the stereoscope next.

Whick. Whack. The monkey in Maudie's hands flipped forward in a somersault, then backward. Violet looked around, trying to trace the sound. Maudie held the little monkey so that her baby sister could see it. *Whick.* The monkey flipped and Violet started, blinking her eyes. *Whack.* The monkey flipped again and Violet laughed out loud. So did Maudie.

Maudie remembered her duty at the window and

Uncle Wilfred's Ear

looked out just in time to see old Mr. Watts's automobile going by.

"Mr. Watts's automobile!" she bellowed, and the boys rushed in from the sitting room to stare out the window until the machine was out of sight.

The next time Maudie looked out, she saw the black top of a buggy moving briskly beyond the bushes far down the road. It began to slow as it neared the Simmses' driveway, and then, when the horse turned in, Maudie yelled, "They're here!" and ran out to the kitchen, pulling up the wrinkles in her stockings. Aunt Sylvie never had wrinkles in *her* stockings, and it was hard to imagine the minister's wife even having legs, for Maudie had never seen so much as an ankle when Sister Bliss took a step.

"Get the sausage, Maudie," her mother instructed quickly. "Peel more potatoes, Claire."

Maudie flew down the cellar steps to fish out some homemade sausages from beneath the thick grease in the crock. Sometimes, when there was company for dinner, children had to wait for "second table." Visitors and parents ate first and sat around talking afterward while Maudie and her brothers and sisters waited in the other room, becoming more starved by the minute. The Blisses, however, always insisted that children be served at the table with them, and when there was chicken, even let them choose the first piece!

Maudie could hear the wheels of the buggy on the lane outside, and the sound of Father going out to tie up the horse. By the time company got through the door, there were always the proper number of plates on the table, so it appeared that the Simmses had been expecting them all along.

This time, however, when Maudie came up with the fat, round sausages, ready for frying, she found not the pastor and his wife and nephew in the kitchen, but her Great-Uncle Wilfred, instead. That was even better!

"Great-Uncle Wilfred!" she screamed happily, running over and hugging his legs. *My little songbird,* he used to call her, because both of them loved to sing. Great-Uncle Wilfred bent down and hugged her, too.

"Wilfred! You just come in here and have yourself some dinner!" Mother shouted. Great-Uncle Wilfred was hard of hearing, and Mother always had to shout.

"Didn't know myself!" he said in answer. "Got up to go to church this morning and the horse set out for Ireton 'fore I knew it." Whenever Wilfred came to dinner unannounced, he blamed it on the horse. He took his favorite chair at the long table

Uncle Wilfred's Ear

---

in the kitchen, Aunt Sylvie fried up the extra sausages, Father asked the blessing, and the meal began.

There were three things that Maudie especially liked about her great-uncle besides his singing: his mustache, which was red in the middle and gray at the ends; his cane, which had a handle carved like the head of a bird; and his ear. Not his real ear. It was something that great Uncle Wilfred carried around with him called a conversation tube, but Wilfred called it his "ear."

It was a long, twisted tube with a rubber tip at one end and a mouthpiece at the other. Whenever Great-Uncle Wilfred wanted to hear something especially well, he would stick the rubber tip in his ear and hold the mouthpiece out toward wherever the sound was coming from. Maudie often had to speak directly into the mouthpiece to be heard at all.

Great-Uncle Wilfred was a book salesman who lived alone in Orange City. The two loves of his life were books and music, and he didn't care what kind of music as long as it was loud. So when dinner was over and the dishes were being done, Great-Uncle Wilfred went into the parlor, where Vernon and Lester took turns winding the phonograph and playing the cylinder records. Loudly. He sat down right next to the talking machine, as Maudie and her brothers called the phonograph.

Lester played "Over the Waves" first, which brought a smile to Great-Uncle Wilfred's face. But when Vernon put on "The Turkish March," Great-Uncle Wilfred tapped his foot and his cane on the floor, both at the same time.

Maudie hurriedly helped Mother and Aunt Sylvie and Claire in the kitchen so that there would be more time in the parlor at the piano. Often when Great-Uncle Wilfred came to visit, he asked one of the children to sing for him. The last time he came, Maudie and Claire sang a duet into his mouth-piece, and Maudie got the giggles so badly she could scarcely finish. But now her voice was ever so much better and she was sure she wouldn't giggle.

When she had finished putting away the pans, Maudie went in and leaned on the arm of Wilfred's chair next to the piano, wishing that he would ask her to sing a song all by herself. When "The Turkish March" was over, however, Wilfred looked at five-year-old Sammy and asked, "How about singing 'Jesus Wants Me for a Sunbeam'?" Sammy sang it earnestly, screwing his face up tight every time he sang "sun-*beam*," which made Uncle Wilfred laugh.

I'll be next, Maudie thought, but then Mother sat down at the piano and the family got ready to sing from the hymn book. Maudie wasn't too disappointed because she liked singing from the hymn book too. Joe was the only one who couldn't carry a tune, so he usually found something to do in the barn when the others gathered around the piano.

It was an American Home piano that Maudie's father had given to Mother at Christmas when Maudie was three. That was the year that one of the Simmses' boy babies had died, and Mother had said she would never get over it. It was then that wonderful Aunt Sylvie had come to live with them to help out. Then Father bought the new piano, and finally—after a long time, after Sammy was born, in fact—Mother got over the sadness.

Now Mrs. Simms sat turning the pages of the hymn book, and Maudie moved still closer to Great-Uncle Wilfred so that it would be her voice he heard loudest through his "ear."

" 'Battle Hymn of the Republic,' " Father called out, choosing the first song.

Maudie liked that one. She loved singing the chorus, especially the "Glory, glory hallelujah," because she could easily hit the high notes. Better than Claire. Almost better than Aunt Sylvie.

"Mine eyes have seen the glory of the coming of the Lord," Father's voice boomed as the hymn began, and when they reached the chorus, Maudie sang very loudly and made her voice wiggle a little, the way Aunt Sylvie's did. She could tell that Claire was looking at her from across the circle. Lester, too. How gorgeous her voice must be!

"Glory, glory, hallelujah!" the family sang again, and when they repeated it the third time—when Maudie made her voice wiggle again on the high note—Mother gently brushed Maudie's arm with her elbow, and Maudie knew exactly what it meant. She had been showing off, and Mother wasn't pleased. The sin of pride, that's what it was. When Sister Bliss sang, for example, her voice was clear and steady. She never allowed even a single wiggle to slip through.

Maudie left before all the songs were over and went out to the barn. Beauty, the Shetland pony that Father had bought the summer before, tossed her head when she saw Maudie, wanting her treat. Maudie hadn't thought to bring one, and stood stroking the pony's nose while Joe worked at mending the bridle.

"Thought you liked singing," he told her.

"I *used* to," she said.

Beauty pushed her muzzle hard against Maudie's arm, trying to search out her pockets for a hidden sweet.

Uncle Wilfred's Ear

"Pa send you out here?" Joe asked.

"No, I just came," Maudie told him.

She climbed up on the side of the stall and lowered herself down onto Beauty's back, where she sat running her fingers through the thick mane. Aunt Sylvie's voice wiggled and nobody seemed to care. Even Claire's was beginning to wiggle and no one scolded. Claire got to wiggle her voice and Sammy got to sing solo, but what did Maudie get, stuck as she was in the middle? Nothing, that's what.

"Joe," she said, "if you could have been born any time you wanted in our family—first, last, or middle—which would you take?"

Joe looked up at her and grinned. "Never thought much about it," he said. "No use worrying over things you can't change, Maudie. Got enough to do with the ones you can."

3

Building Pictures

The worst part of it all was that they hadn't even missed her, not even Aunt Sylvie. When Maudie went in the house later, the singing was over and Great-Uncle Wilfred was showing the boys his new folding compass. There were so many people in the room, in fact, that if they had known she was gone, they didn't realize she was back.

So Maudie sat around waiting for Monday. She liked school because she loved her teacher, Miss

Richardson. The teacher never once forgot that Maudie was there.

Of course, it was Miss Richardson's job to pay attention to children. Her day wasn't taken up with cooking, baking, and sewing the way that Mother's was. But it almost seemed to Maudie as though her teacher knew what she was thinking without her even having to ask. Maudie had already decided that she wanted to be a teacher when she grew up, just like Miss Richardson.

It was cold on Monday, and as the days wore on, it grew colder still, as though winter were just beginning. Mother started heating bricks in the oven again, wrapping them in towels so that each child could carry one to bed to warm the sheets. Even then, when Maudie woke up on Friday, the blanket around her head was frozen stiff from her breath.

Maudie and Claire shared a small room at the top of the stairs, and the rest of the second floor was a bedroom for the boys. There was a floor register next to Sammy's bed, which brought warm air up from the kitchen. But Maudie and Claire's room was so cold that ice sometimes formed a half-inch thick on the inside of the window pane.

Maudie felt the straw mattress rise as her sister got out of bed. She rolled over sleepily into the warm space Claire had left behind, and watched her sister dress. Claire had skin like Aunt Sylvie's and Mother's—"speckled like a bird's egg," Father called it. Maudie had a few freckles too, but she looked more like her father with his brown hair and eyes. She waited until Claire had pulled on her shirtwaist and skirt and then, after Claire fled downstairs where it was warm to wash her face and comb her hair, Maudie worked at getting up.

"One, two, three, *go!*" she whispered, but her legs wouldn't move. "One, two, three, *go!*" Maudie counted again, and this time she forced her feet over the edge of the mattress, sucking in her breath as they hit the cold floor. She threw off her night-gown and—skin covered with goose bumps—reached for her underwear with the long legs and sleeves.

Maudie wished that she had gone to bed the night before wearing her underwear beneath her night-gown, as she often did in winter. Now she made a game of dressing to keep from thinking about the cold. Grabbing her black stockings and garters, she tried to get them all on before she could recite the first verse of "Onward Christian Soldiers": "OnwardChristian-soldiers, marchingastowar . . ." Then came her cotton bloomers with elastic at the waist and knees, her petticoat, her dress, and finally Maudie thrust her arms through the cotton apron that she wore over her dress. Grabbing her shoes and the button hook, she rushed downstairs and sat by the warmth of the kitchen stove while she put them on. Eleven buttons up the side of each high-top leather shoe. Maudie stuck the little hook through each buttonhole, one at a time, grasped the button with it, and pulled the hook back through the hole, bringing the button along.

Violet, the baby, and five-year-old Sammy were still asleep, but everyone else was crowded into the kitchen. Father and Joe had been up working long before daybreak, and now they wanted breakfast.

While Claire and Aunt Sylvie made the lunches, packing thick sandwiches securely down into the syrup pails that the children used as lunch buckets, Mother stood at the table dishing out fried potatoes and toast to each plate. Claire was going through eighth grade twice because there wasn't any grade above it in the one-room school they all attended. Next year she would probably stay home with Aunt Sylvie and Mother because the high school, in Hawarden, was eleven miles away, much too far for Father to take her there each day in the wagon. Joe had already stopped going to school and worked all day with Father on the farm.

"It's got the look of snow," Mother said later as they put on their coats. "Take scarves with you."

Maudie and Lester followed behind Claire and Vernon on the mile-and-a-quarter walk to school— one foot on the road, the other in the frozen grass— syrup pails clanking occasionally, one against the other, as they went. Maudie longed for spring— longed to take off the underwear that made her perspire, longed for the very first day she could go barefoot in the yard. By the time they reached the school, however, a snowflake had landed on her cheek.

Inside, there was even a thin layer of ice in the water bucket, the dipper caught at a strange angle in the center. Maudie kept her coat on until the wood stove had heated the classroom, then hung the coat in the cloakroom with the others. All day the snow came down, so heavy at times that it was difficult to see out the windows. Twice Miss Richardson had to send a boy to shovel a path to the girls' outhouse in back and another path to the boys'. And still the snow wouldn't stop. Maudie didn't care. She wouldn't have minded if she had been snowed in all weekend with Miss Richardson, especially because today was Friday, and the teacher made Fridays special.

The other children felt it too, and moved quickly through the day's routine. While the first graders went to the recitation bench at the front of the room, the four second graders copied their spelling words from the blackboard onto their slates. While Maudie began her multiplication numbers, the three boys in the fourth-grade row read their history books. There were no fifth graders at all, five in sixth, no seventh graders, and three boys in eighth with Claire, studying geography and physiology. Some of the desks were double, and friends often sat together. But because Maudie was the only member of the third grade, she had to sit alone.

One of the first graders was reciting at Miss Richardson's desk: "The . . . dog . . . has . . . a . . ." And Maudie remembered that at the end of the sentence there was a picture of a bone. When *she* was in first grade, she used to reach for Miss Richardson's long watch chain and wind it slowly around her ear while she recited. Miss Richardson never seemed to mind.

At three o'clock, the teacher finally said the words they had all been waiting for: "It's time," she told them, smiling, "for building pictures."

It was as though a giant dust mop had suddenly swept the room clean. Desk tops that had been cluttered before were suddenly clear; papers that had been scattered about appeared in a neat stack on Miss Richardson's desk. Maudie sat with her hands folded.

Maudie in the Middle

Choose me, she thought earnestly, staring straight into her teacher's eyes. *Please, please, double please, choose me.*

And as though the thought had jumped straight out of her own head and into the teacher's, Miss Richardson said, "Maudie Mae, would you like to be 'it'?"

Maudie was not at all surprised, but she beamed happily as she rose from her seat.

"Heads down," said Miss Richardson, and instantly all heads dropped to the desktops, all eyes closed, while Maudie moved softly about the room, tapping three other children on the head. She chose Vernon, Anne Hubbell, and a small boy in the first grade. Silently they went to the front of the room, and Maudie arranged them into a "picture": Vernon with his hands over his eyes, Anne with her hands over her ears, and the first grader with his hands over his mouth. *See no evil, hear no evil, speak no evil.* Then Maudie tiptoed back to her seat.

"Heads up!" called Miss Richardson, and when the class had looked for only two seconds, she called, "Heads down." The three children at the front of the room scampered noiselessly back to their seats. Maudie giggled. And at the "Heads up" call again, the class tried to remember who had been at the front of the room and how they'd been arranged.

Building Pictures

27

It was always fun to see what was remembered, and how mixed-up things could get. Someone even thought that Maudie herself had been up front, forgetting that she had been the one who was "it."

The first one who guessed correctly got to be "it" the next time around. Maudie put her head down and closed her eyes, hoping for that familiar tap on the head. By the time the afternoon was over, almost everyone had been chosen to "build a picture" at least once, and it seemed that the game had hardly begun before it was time to go home. As Maudie pulled on her coat, she saw her father sitting in the big wagon sled outside, his shoulders hunched against the wind, the breath of the horses a cloud of steam about their heads.

"Today is a perfect day!" she told Miss Richardson as she put on her mittens.

The teacher smiled down at her. "Is it, Maudie? We certainly don't get many of those in a lifetime. I hope you enjoy your perfect day."

The children spilled out the door, and Maudie tumbled into the wagon sled with her brothers and two neighbors who lived along the way, while Claire chose to sit more sedately up on the seat beside her father. There was straw in the back of the wagon and horse blankets as well. When the last leg was over the side, the last arm buried beneath the straw,

Maudie's father gave the reins a shake, and at his "Giddap," the horses moved off toward home.

Snug there in the straw, Maudie simply could not stop smiling. If she could "build her own picture" of being happy, she would arrange some children just as they were then—in the back of a wagon with runners, weighted down with heavy blankets, snow blowing about their faces. She watched the flakes swirling down at her from overhead, and hoped it would be a long, long time before she felt old enough to have to sit on the seat with her father.

4

The Time of the Pox

The trouble with Maudie was that after every *good* thing that happened, just when she was feeling best about herself, she did something to "upset the apple-cart," as Aunt Sylvie put it.

It all began that weekend. Not what Maudie did, exactly—that came three weeks later—but it started with the snow, seven inches of it on the ground. Later, Maudie blamed what she did on Lester's sickness, and she blamed the sickness on the snow. But this Saturday morning, when she looked out the window and saw it glistening in the sun, she thought, mistakenly, that this was the start of a wonderful weekend. Claire, Vernon, Maudie, Lester, and Sammy took the bobsled and set out for the hill beyond the south pasture.

It wasn't a steep hill, but it was long, and usually, by the time the bobsled reached the bottom, everyone on board was screaming, Maudie loudest of all. They would plunge through the gap in the barbed-wire fence and skid across the frozen creek before tumbling off, top-heavy in sweaters, coats, caps, and scarves. Then they would set off again up the hill.

On this particular day, however, Claire was grumpy as they walked to the hill because Joe hadn't come along. Twice now, Joe had been too busy with work on the farm to go with them, and this always upset her, because it was Joe who got the younger ones lined up right on the sled, Joe who kept things lively.

"Not much fun going sledding if it's always got to be me leading the parade," she complained, and then, "Hurry up, Sammy!" as she turned to wait for the youngest. She seemed sorry afterward, but then turned around and did it again; and Sammy, up to his knees in snow, puffed even harder, trying to keep up.

The Time of the Pox

The first ride down the hill was Claire's last. There was a crazy argument at the top as to who would sit where; and then, when they shoved off at last and Claire was trying to maneuver them safely through the two sections of barbed wire, Maudie nervously grabbed hold of Claire's legs on either side of her. As she did so, she accidentally unhooked some of the buttons on Claire's leggings, which tightly covered each of Claire's legs to keep her warm.

"You *always* do that!" Claire yelled at her when they reached the bottom. "You always unhook my leggings, and then I have to button them all over again."

"I'll do it for you," Maudie said quickly. She didn't *always* unbutton Claire's leggings when they were sledding, just some of the time. But it was the excuse Claire needed to leave, and she marched back toward the house.

"I hope I *never* grow up!" Sammy said darkly as they watched her go, arms swinging stiffly at her sides.

It wasn't as much fun on the hill with just the four of them, especially without Joe. After a while Lester complained that his toes were cold, and then, when Sammy snagged his coat on the barbed wire, they all decided to go home.

Taking off their galoshes on the back porch where the milk cans gave off a sour smell, Maudie could hear Mother and Aunt Sylvie talking in the kitchen as they kneaded the bread.

"She's growing up," Aunt Sylvie was saying. "Things that used to be fun for her aren't so wonderful anymore."

So Sammy had been right, Maudie thought. It was growing up that was Claire's problem. She heard her mother sigh.

"Claire's not going to take so easily to staying home with us," she said. "Joe just seemed to slide right out of eighth grade and into his work on the farm. I don't know what this kitchen's going to be like with Claire in it all day."

Maybe being one of the older children in a family wasn't as wonderful as she had thought, Maudie decided. Maybe only the very youngest had the most fun. *She* had been one of the youngest once, and Maudie tried to remember what that was like. She could hardly remember it at all.

It was the next morning that Lester took sick with fever. Mother stayed home from church to care for him, but when Maudie and the others returned from the service, there was a strange buggy in the yard. Mother met them at the door to say that Lester was worse and the doctor had come.

The Time of the Pox

33

The black wall telephone in the kitchen never looked as scary to Maudie as it did when someone was sick. Father had it put in two years ago, just in case they needed the doctor in a hurry, and Maudie never quite got over the feeling that a ringing telephone meant trouble.

Aunt Sylvie moved silently about the kitchen, putting an extra plate on the table for the doctor, while Mother and Father went upstairs where Lester was being examined. Maudie sat with her brothers and Claire in the sitting room, her eyes on the stairs. She knew they were all thinking about sledding the day before—how Lester had been the first one to get cold, and that maybe they should have come home sooner.

When the doctor came down again, he did not stay for dinner but got in his buggy and drove off. Mother stood at the window, one hand on her cheek, watching him go.

"Mama?" Maudie said softly, going over and nudging her arm. "What is it?"

"Smallpox," Mother said, and her hand traveled down her neck until it reached the top button on her dress. Her fingers gripped it hard.

Maudie didn't know exactly how serious smallpox was, but she knew that someone would be out from the board of health to nail a quarantine sign on the door. A quarantine sign meant that no one could leave the farm for the next few weeks, and no one outside the family could come into the house.

Violet came down with it next. There was fever first and vomiting, and on the third day large crops of small pink spots appeared on her face and arms and body, just as they had with Lester. Mother tied mittens to Violet's hands so she wouldn't scratch, and went from Violet to Lester with cold, wet cloths for the forehead.

April Fool's Day came and went without a single trick being played on anyone. Last year, just after breakfast, Father had sent Lester to a neighbor's to borrow a handsaw and a "round square." Lester, still groggy with sleep, had climbed on his pony and set off, and the family whooped with laughter when he returned, puzzled, carrying a handsaw and a slice of bread, which Mrs. Wheeler made round by cutting the corners off.

On the fifth day, when Maudie got the pox, Aunt Sylvie, Vernon, and Sammy came down with it too, so that when it was Maudie's turn to have her mother sing to her and rub her back and place wet cloths on her forehead, Mother was caring for Aunt Sylvie, and it was Claire who had to do it for Maudie. By now, however, there were so many sick people in the family that the ones who were well didn't have enough hands to do all they should. It was miraculous, Mother said later, that no one died, and that Aunt Sylvie and the girls got through it without their faces being much scarred.

To Maudie, though, the worst part of the pox was not the scars or even the days she was sickest, but the time near the end of the quarantine when everyone was getting better. The novelty had worn off, and everyone was tired of being inside. Even the boys were fidgeting to get back to school. A peddler came all the way up the lane to sell extracts, saw the quarantine sign on the door, and turned right around again. Maudie would have liked to let him in just to have someone else to talk to.

It was fun at first, of course. When it began to look as though the ones who had smallpox would be all right, and the ones who didn't have it—Father, Joe, Claire, and Mother—wouldn't get it at all, they began looking at the quarantine as a kind of vacation. Joe teased by sprinkling pepper on the hot stove and making them all sneeze. Even Father took it easier, loping about the house, stopping to play with Violet as she munched cookies in her high chair.

"Here's a pox," he would say, pointing to a scar on her arm and tickling her there, "and here's a pox," tickling her cheek, "and *here's* a pox!" he would say at last, tickling her hard on the tummy, and Violet would squeal with laughter.

When Aunt Sylvie recovered, she did her best to entertain the others. She took a big square crackerbox, cut it into pieces, and made a deck of cards for PIT. Maudie and Claire and their brothers sat at the table for hours, shouting "Two, two, two!" or "Three, three, three!" and sometimes screaming "Corner!" on whatever grain made up their entire hand. When they tired of that, they made vinegar taffy, put traps in every room to catch the mice, and went through all the pictures for the stereoscope, even the ones of the Crucifixion and Christ's early life. But the day before the quarantine was over, everyone seemed to be out of patience entirely. Aunt Sylvie scolded Maudie sharply for something Vernon had done; Sammy sassed Mother; Father took the buggy into town when he was clearly supposed to wait one more day, and Claire, who was sewing a dress, couldn't get the sleeves right and snapped at everyone who came near her.

It was on a day like this that Maudie might have done something to help soothe the family back into a good humor. It was a time she might have helped look after Violet and Sammy to take some of the

The Time of the Pox

burden off her mother and aunt. Instead—that afternoon—Maudie did something she knew she was not allowed to do.

The black telephone on the kitchen wall was a party line, and Maudie knew all the other rings and who they were for. One long ring was central. The Simmses' ring was one long, three shorts, and one long; the Wheelers' was two longs and three shorts; Mrs. Franklin's was three shorts and two longs; and old Mr. Watts's was one long and four shorts. . . . Maudie knew them all. And so, at about three in the afternoon, when Aunt Sylvie was in the sitting room rocking Violet, Mother was lying down, and the others were scattered around the house being crabby, Mrs. Wheeler's ring sounded, and after it had stopped, Maudie softly tiptoed over to the telephone and listened in.

She didn't just listen in, however. There was something about Maudie Mae that seemed to invite trouble—to call attention to herself even if it meant a scolding. Sometimes it seemed as though she weren't content to "upset the applecart," but had to upset the universe as well. And so, after Mrs. Wheeler and Mrs. Franklin had discussed babies, croup, and the wonders of camphorated oil, and had turned to spring dresses, Maudie just had to let them know that someone was listening.

Maudie in the Middle

"I'm thinking of French silk in yellow or blue," Mrs. Franklin said. "What do you think, Esther?"

"Green," said Maudie softly.

"What?" asked Mrs. Franklin. "I look terrible in green!"

"I didn't say that," said Mrs. Wheeler. "I think blue would go best with your eyes."

"Green," said Maudie again, holding back a giggle.

Mrs. Franklin sighed. "There's someone else on this line, and I've got a good notion who."

Maudie's heart pounded, but she didn't hang up. How could they *possibly* know it was she?

"There are certain children around here who have no manners at all," Mrs. Wheeler agreed loudly.

Maybe they thought she was someone else, Maudie decided. Maybe they thought she was Anne Hubbell. She gently blew her breath into the mouthpiece and heard it come back in her ear as a hiss.

"As I was saying . . . ," Mrs. Wheeler went on.

"Green," said Maudie again, and this time she giggled out loud.

"I'm going straight to Mrs. Hubbell and tell her what that child is up to," said Mrs. Wheeler, and Maudie's heart raced even faster. They *did* think

The Time of the Pox

she was Anne. "If she were *my* daughter, I'd take the hairbrush to her right quick."

"Green," said Maudie, and then her tongue seemed to stick to the roof of her mouth, because there in the doorway stood her father. Maudie hung up.

But Father walked over and lifted the receiver again.

"Hello," he said to the two women who were still on the line. "This is Tom Simms and I think my daughter Maudie wants to apologize." He handed the receiver to her.

Maudie felt her ears turning red, swelling until they seemed to stick out like the handles of a sugar bowl. Aunt Sylvie had come to the door of the kitchen now and stood watching. Maudie backed away, shaking her head, looking at Father in horror. He reached out and put the receiver in her hand, closing her fingers around it.

Swallowing, Maudie stepped up to the mouthpiece. "I'm sorry," she said, then dropped the receiver and fled upstairs.

She lay face down on her bed until supper. Later, at family worship in the parlor, Mother read the Scripture and Father led in prayer. Maudie got down on her knees by the sofa with the others, her forehead resting on her hands, her sleeve touch-

Maudie in the Middle

ing Aunt Sylvie's, and listened as Father prayed that all his children might do unto others as they would have others do unto them. Maudie knew that he was talking about her in particular.

If she had learned her lesson—if she was certain she would never listen in on a phone conversation again—she'd feel better. But Maudie knew, even as she knelt there, that there were other applecarts to be upset, before she even began to discover why.

The Time of the Pox

5

Waiting for Sears, Roebuck

Spring came when they least expected it. For a week, it seemed, it had rained every day, and Maudie sloshed to school beside the others, heads down, water running along the sleeves of their rubber raincoats, dripping off the cuffs, and sliding down the sides of their lunch pails. And then one morning Maudie went out to feed the chickens and there it was—the wind soft against her face. On the way back from school that day the children unbuttoned their coats and arrived home with sleeves flopping, chasing each other like young pups.

They had been waiting until it was warm enough to hitch the Shetland pony up to the cart, remembering the summer before when Beauty had patiently pulled them around the yard. But this year Beauty was expecting a foal, so they put it off, knowing she could not pull them until she had delivered and grown strong once more.

On the night she gave birth, however, Beauty died. While Joe and Vernon and Father dug a pit beyond the haystack to bury Beauty, and Claire and Sammy wept, Maudie sat on the back stoop, her eyes stinging, holding the new foal in a blanket. Its long legs were buckled under, the fine hair on its body still damp. Maudie knew that she was holding the cause of Beauty's death in her arms, yet she couldn't hate the foal. So she hated instead what had happened, and held the newborn close.

"We'll call him Lucky," she announced to Claire, who was still dabbing at her eyes with her apron. "Lucky to be alive. That's what Mother says."

They carried Lucky about like a baby, passing him from one child to another. Maudie even took him upstairs and let him lie for a while on her

Waiting for Sears, Roebuck

bed. Every few hours he needed a bottle of milk, and Mother even got up in the middle of the night to get it.

When it came time to wean him from the bottle, Father showed them how he weaned the calves. He put a pail of milk in front of the foal, then dipped a finger in and let him suck. Again he dipped his hand and offered a finger to Lucky, but this time, when the foal thrust out his muzzle, ready to suck, Father plunged his hand back into the pail and the foal's head followed. It came back up, snorting and snuffling, its nose covered with milk.

Maudie laughed delightedly. "Let me try!" she said, and then they all had to try it. Lucky almost upset the milk bucket, but he learned. Sometimes, right in the middle of their play, Maudie would remember she was not thinking of Beauty at all. But then, because Lucky was a part of Beauty, she knew that it was all right.

"I'm not wearing *these* any longer!" Claire said one morning as she was dressing, and dropped her long underwear in a heap in one corner. Maudie tumbled out of bed to dump *her* long underwear on top of it, laughing.

How strange and cool it felt to have her cotton bloomers next to her skin again, to slide her black stockings up the calves of her legs without having to tug them up over the wrinkled, lumpy legs of her long underwear.

At school, with a warm breeze blowing through the window, Miss Richardson began reading *The Mysterious Key* aloud to the class to keep their attention.

"Just one more chapter," they pleaded each time she set the book aside. But even then, when recess came, they were out the door like a shot, running like crazed hens about the schoolyard, shedding their coats, searching out the sheep sorrel that grew at the edge of the pasture. Maudie sat in the grass in the sun chewing the sour weed, eager to eat something green, and later picked a bunch to take back home to Aunt Sylvie.

It was when the trees began to blossom that Maudie learned about goodness—that, just as it takes very little sometimes to turn a bad day into a worse one, to upset the applecart and everything in it, it sometimes did not take much, either, to make it good. It all started with Sears, Roebuck.

Father sold a load of hogs in Ireton, so Mother said that the family could place an order with Sears, Roebuck. Maudie wasn't sure which she liked best—Christmas or Sears. Whenever Father sold a load of hogs or cattle, Mother took out the mail-order

Waiting for Sears, Roebuck

45

catalog and everyone got to order. Father always grumbled that they bought too much, but Mother only clucked her tongue and reminded him of all the things they needed that they *weren't* going to buy, so she usually got her way.

It was almost as much fun looking through the catalog as it was waiting for the things to come. The catalog was always in someone's lap, and by the time it got to Maudie, the pages were earmarked and dirty, but she didn't care. Maudie would sit by the kerosene lamp in the parlor, holding the big book on her knees, studying the models on the pages in their lawn dresses or capes or leggings or underwear. Sears, Roebuck used real photographs of people's heads for their models, and then an artist would draw the rest of the body. Sometimes the heads weren't attached quite right to the shoulders, and Maudie would suddenly come across a lady in a sailor dress whose neck was too far to the right. Maudie would move her own head sideways to see if this were possible, and hurry on to the next page.

There were so many things to buy that it was hard to make a choice: patent leather shoes with buckles, folding fans of Chinese silk, musical dolls, bird whistles, toy tea sets and sewing machines, playing cards, trumpets, combs, clocks. . . .

"Now order whatever you want, Sylvie," Mother always told her sister, partly, Maudie supposed, because Aunt Sylvie was such a help to her in the house. This time Aunt Sylvie ordered a hat.

"Which do you think, Maudie?" she asked, pointing to three different pictures of women, each wearing a hat larger than the one before.

Maudie's heart beat faster. Aunt Sylvie was asking *her!*

"This one," said Maudie, pointing to the most expensive hat on the page. *Fine summer leghorn,* the catalog said, *with imported silk poppies, only $4.75.* "You would be *beautiful* in it, Aunt Sylvie!"

"That's just the one I had my eye on," her aunt said, and marked the number down. She also ordered some red stockings with white polka dots.

It was a week before everyone could make up their minds and the order went off to Chicago. Maudie ordered a 30¢-bottle of lilac cologne, a silk hair ribbon, a beaded coin purse, and a bank that looked like a little brick building.

Then the long wait began. Every time the phone rang, they all scrambled to answer. And when it did not ring all day, either Maudie, Claire, or Vernon would crank the handle to call the freight agent in Ireton and ask if a shipment had come in for Tom Simms.

Waiting for Sears, Roebuck

The weather, which had been rainy some weeks before, turned dry, and as the men worked the fields, huge clouds of dust rolled in toward the house, seeping through the doors and windows and covering the chairs, tables—even the telephone—with a thin film. Maudie would wipe off the telephone in the morning and by afternoon it would need dusting still again.

She lived in delicious anticipation. Even her most hated chore—emptying the chamber pots beneath each bed—did not seem so awful, knowing that any day now the freight agent might phone up and say that the shipment was there. She would run the chamber pots to the outhouse and back again as fast as she could, just in case the phone should ring. She did not even *think* of listening in on the telephone. It did not seem very hard to be good while waiting for something wonderful to happen.

And then, one Thursday when Maudie called down, the agent said yes.

"What?" said Maudie.

"Yes," the agent said. "The order for Tom Simms, thank the Lord in heaven, has come."

What yelling and excitement! Since Joe and Father were out in the fields, Mother said that Vernon could take the horses and wagon to Ireton to pick up the order.

Maudie in the Middle

That evening, the dinner dishes had never been done faster nor the kitchen cleaned as quickly. Everyone helped, and as soon as the last saucepan was put away in the cupboard, Sammy and Lester pulled the chairs out into a circle while Joe and Vernon hoisted the large wooden crate in from the back porch. Mother got the hammer from the drawer and handed it to Father, and when the lid was off, Lester and Maudie dived into the excelsior to lift out first one thing, then another.

The large objects were the easiest to find—two cans of gray paint, the banquet lamp for Mother, a new chisel, and of course Aunt Sylvie's hatbox. Everyone stopped to watch while Aunt Sylvie placed the hat, with the orange poppies against white silk, on her head. She *was* beautiful in it, just as Maudie had said, and Maudie raced to her room for a little mirror so that Sylvie could see for herself.

But the boys were soon digging again, looking for the jumping frog for Sammy, the rubber balls, the watch for Joe, the backgammon game—whistles and warships, tops, and even a little toy cash register. Excelsior was all over the floor but nobody cared.

Maudie took her own treasures into the parlor to enjoy them one by one. The beaded coin purse wasn't quite as pretty as it had looked in the catalog, and Sears had sent the wrong color ribbon, but

Waiting for Sears, Roebuck

the little bank was lovely and so was the lilac cologne. She dabbed a little cologne behind each ear as she had seen Aunt Sylvie do. Out in the kitchen, Mother and Aunt Sylvie were laughing together over Sylvie's red stockings with the white polka dots.

"Wherever will you wear those, Sylvie?" Mother asked her.

"I'll think of someplace," Sylvie said, and they laughed again.

The next day, Maudie made her wear them on a visit to the plum tree at the back of the meadow, Aunt Sylvie's favorite place on the farm.

"No one will see them but me," Maudie told her, so Aunt Sylvie put the red stockings on just for fun, and Maudie followed after her on the path, laughing each time Aunt Sylvie lifted her dress and the stockings showed red on her ankles. The path twisted and turned. At the very end, the blossoms were in full bloom on the plum tree. Maudie and her aunt sat beneath the branches, their ankles crossed, Maudie in her black stockings, Aunt Sylvie in her red ones with the white polka dots, her arm around Maudie's shoulders.

Maudie decided that if ever Aunt Sylvie was going to ask her to be her godchild, this was the perfect time.

"This is *my* favorite place on the farm, too!" she

said, leaning her head against Aunt Sylvie's arm. "Everything *you* like, *I* like!"

Aunt Sylvie just smiled and gently wound a lock of Maudie's hair around one finger.

"That's because we're special to each other, aren't we?" Maudie went on, wishing she could sit there, in exactly that way, with Aunt Sylvie's fingers in her hair, forever.

"Of course," Aunt Sylvie said.

"*Really* special?" Maudie asked.

"*Really* special," said Aunt Sylvie.

Maudie waited. Bees buzzed, and in the distance Maudie could see Joe harrowing the west field. When two minutes had gone by, however, and then three, Maudie stole a look at her aunt. Aunt Sylvie was sitting with her head against the trunk of the plum tree, eyes closed, face tipped up toward the sun.

"I wonder," said Maudie at last, "what would ever happen to me if Mama died."

Aunt Sylvie's eyes opened slowly, but she did not look down. "What a sad thought, Maudie, on such a beautiful day!"

"I know, but I worry about who would take care of me and love me always."

"We would *all* take care of you and love you always," said Aunt Sylvie.

Waiting for Sears, Roebuck

51

"I mean, who would take care of me and be my mother?"

Aunt Sylvie's eyes closed again, she smiled, and gave Maudie's hair a little tug. "Now *that*," she said, "would be up to your father to decide."

Maudie leaned thoughtfully against her aunt again. Maybe you had to have your father's permission before you could be somebody's godchild. She would ask him the very first chance that she got.

She tried not to wiggle too much beside Aunt Sylvie so that her aunt would not even think about going back to the house. Sometimes, when it rained in the night—*really* rained, with lightning and thunder something awful—Maudie would creep downstairs to crawl into bed in the guest room beside Aunt Sylvie. As long as she lay still, Maudie discovered, Aunt Sylvie would allow her to stay there, snuggled up, but if she squirmed about too much, Aunt Sylvie would give her a pat and suggest it was time she went back to the bed she shared with Claire. Maudie had learned to lie very, very still. Even when she had an itch. Even when the itch was on her foot and she could not possibly reach it.

It was the following day that Maudie's goodness was put to the test. Some of the toys had broken already, and Lester was sulking because he wished he'd ordered something else. When Maudie walked into the parlor, she found him holding her lilac cologne.

"Lah dee dah dee dah!" Lester sang, waltzing around with the bottle.

"You *give* me that!" Maudie demanded.

Lester laughed and took out the glass stopper at the top. He held the bottle high in the air, tipping it ever so slightly and watching Maudie's face.

"*Give* me that!" she yelled again.

At that moment, the bottle tipped a little too much, and a stream of cologne poured down onto Lester's overalls. Maudie grabbed the bottle in time to save the rest, and Lester fled through the kitchen, out the door, and hightailed it for the barn.

Maudie sat down, holding the bottle, and tried to think what Sister Bliss would do. *Return evil with good,* came to mind, but Maudie didn't trust herself. She knew that however much she tried, she wasn't good enough yet to do something kind for Lester in return for spilling her cologne. To keep herself from doing something awful, in fact, was about as much as she could hope for. She took all of her things up to her room, put them away in her dresser drawer, and sat down on her bed to think about goodness.

As she sat there by the window, she could see

Waiting for Sears, Roebuck

Lester hiding behind the barn, peering out every so often to see if she were coming. After a long time, he made a run for the machine shed, then hid behind the door, peeping out again to see why Maudie hadn't come.

Maudie began to smile. She sat on the bed a long time, watching Lester sneaking from shed to outhouse, from tree to tree. Once he lifted the bib of his overalls to his nose and took a sniff, then turned his face away. Maudie laughed out loud. She knew that as much as Lester wanted to come inside and change clothes, he wouldn't dare. All Maudie was doing was sitting up in her room, minding her own business, while Lester crept around outside, watching the door.

He didn't come near her all day. When Maudie came out at all, Lester would take off running in the opposite direction. He spent the afternoon out in the heat of the fields with Father, afraid to come any closer.

About five o'clock, the wind changed to the northeast and now the dust really billowed in, great swirls of it rolling across the lawn and the clearing. Lester came in at last for his supper, his skin covered with dust, his overalls reeking, and Vernon and Joe teased him about how he must have a girlfriend, all that perfume on his clothes.

Maudie in the Middle

Maudie said nothing. She sat on her side of the table next to Aunt Sylvie with her hands in her lap, as good as she ever imagined she could be. Maybe what Sister Bliss taught her in Sunday School was true, that goodness was its own reward. It certainly seemed so that day.

6

Maudie in the Middle

Just as one bad thing seemed to follow on the heels of another, sometimes good things came in pairs as well. Shortly after the Sears, Roebuck order arrived, for example, it was time for the annual box social at school.

This was one of Aunt Sylvie's favorite events of the year. Maudie liked box socials too, but not as much as Aunt Sylvie did. This year Claire was packing a box of her own, and the family seemed to make a big thing out of that. It had something to do with men and boyfriends. That much Maudie knew.

She sat at the kitchen table watching while Mother and Aunt Sylvie and Claire each packed a box. Mother put enough food in her hamper for the whole family, and Father always bid on her box because he knew there would be a butterscotch pie inside. But Claire and Aunt Sylvie only packed enough in their boxes for two people. Maudie noticed the chocolate cake that Aunt Sylvie was putting inside hers.

"I want to eat with Aunt Sylvie," she said. Mother and Aunt Sylvie only laughed.

When Mother put the lid on her hamper, she tied a big blue bow on one side. Claire put a fancy bird's nest on hers, with three small blue sugar eggs and a little felt bird inside it. But Aunt Sylvie tied her box up with pink and purple ribbons, and purple silk roses on top. It would be the most beautiful box at the social, Maudie thought, to match beautiful Aunt Sylvie.

The social was held on Saturday afternoon, and there were so many buggies around the school that the playground was full. There were three automobiles too, and Joe and Vernon and Maudie lingered outside with their friends, looking over the automobiles and deciding which ones they would buy when they were grown.

"Good-weather machines, that's all they are," one of the boys said to Joe. "Okay for a day when the roads are dry, but you get out in the mud with one, you'd give anything for a good strong horse."

Maudie let them chatter and followed the others inside. To her, the most exciting part of a box social was the program beforehand. Every child in the school had a song to sing or a poem to recite, and beaming parents sat at the back of the room while their children performed in front. The long table heaped with lunches gave off an assorted fragrance of chicken, ham, and turkey.

Miss Richardson was dressed in a lace shirtwaist with a brown skirt and a brown silk rose at her throat. Maudie watched as she moved about the room, greeting people and telling them how the money from the sale of the lunches would be used to buy more books for the bookshelf.

That's what I'll be like some day, Maudie told herself. She would have a brown silk rose at *her* throat, and she would clap loudly after each child had performed, just as Miss Richardson did.

The program began with the first graders singing

a song about a windmill, Vernon playing "Turkey in the Straw" on his harmonica, Claire playing the piano, and two of the sixth-grade boys telling riddles. Both Lester and Maudie were reciting poems by James Whitcomb Riley. Lester's poem was "Naughty Claude," about a boy who wouldn't say thank-you to his ma, and when Lester forgot how the fifth line went, Maudie had to whisper it to him. No one seemed to mind.

Finally it was Maudie's turn. She stood up in front of the large crowd, her hair freshly curled with mother's stove-heated curling iron, the ruffle on the hem of her dress so starched that she couldn't see her shoes beneath it. For two weeks she had practiced saying her poem in the sitting room while Mother sewed. Mother had suggested just where Maudie might raise the pitch of her voice and what gestures she could use to make it more dramatic.

"'A Life Lesson,' by James Whitcomb Riley," Maudie said. She could see both Mother and Aunt Sylvie watching her from one side, Miss Richardson watching from the other. Vernon and Joe and some of the older boys stood at the back of the room grinning. Maudie fixed her eyes on Violet, who was sitting on Father's lap, playing with his straw hat.

Maudie in the Middle

"There! little girl; don't cry!
They have broken your doll, I know. . . ."

Maudie lowered her head and rubbed her eyes sorrowfully. When she recited the second verse, about the broken slate, she let her lips quiver and paid no attention to Vernon's muffled snicker. And when she got to the little girl's broken heart in the third verse, she lifted her eyes to the window and stared bravely out at the sky.

She had done it! For once she had actually done something perfectly—all three verses. Maudie made a little bow and went back to sit with her family. Everyone clapped loudly and was still clapping when she sat down. If only this moment could go on and on forever, Maudie thought. Mother smiled down the row at her. Father too, and Aunt Sylvie reached over and squeezed her hand. Maudie remembered how happy she had been that day in the wagon sled, covered with straw, the snow coming down around her, and decided that this was even better. *This* was undoubtedly the happiest she had ever been, and she would remember it always.

She was so happy, in fact, that she couldn't sit still, and when the raffle of the lunch boxes began, Maudie slipped outside with the other children. The auctioneer would hold up each box, one at a time, and the men and older boys were supposed to bid on them. When the box was sold to the highest bidder, the buyer would go up to the front and get it, and afterward the woman or girl who had made the lunch would go outside with him to eat it. Husbands usually bought their wives' baskets, but the single men didn't know to whom the other boxes belonged, and there was always a lot of surprised laughter.

Maudie was still in a frenzy of excitement because her piece had gone so well. She went racing around between the parked buggies playing tag with the other children. She had run twice around old Mr. Watts's automobile when she suddenly found herself face-to-face with a stocky, red-haired man. Horace Benson. Maudie skidded to a stop.

Horace Benson was younger than Father, but old enough to have a bald spot beginning at the top of his head. Although he had a marvelous bass voice, he opened his mouth so wide when he sang that he could easily swallow a baseball, Father always said. Only a week ago at the Sunday evening hymn-sing, as the congregation was singing "When the Roll is Called up Yonder," Maudie and Lester had peeped over the back of their pew to watch Horace Benson sing. He opened his mouth so wide on "Roo-oll" and "Yoo-onder," that they ducked down in

Maudie in the Middle

the seat, laughing. Maudie was sure that Mr. Benson wanted to speak to her about their laughing. But he didn't.

"Maudie!" he said, and smiled. "That was certainly a beautiful box your Aunt Sylvie made for the social."

Maudie stared at him.

"Did you help her make it?"

Maudie shook her head.

"Well, I don't think I've seen a larger red ribbon in my life."

Maudie stared some more. "Hers doesn't have a red ribbon. It's got pink and purple ribbons on the sides."

"Oh!" Horace Benson's mouth opened wide. "Oh!" he said again, and Maudie hoped she wouldn't laugh. "The one with the velvet bows in the corners, then!"

"No, not that one!" Maudie told him. "It has pink and purple ribbons on the sides and purple silk roses on top. It looks like a hat."

"Oh!" Horace said again. "*That* one! The prettiest box there, I swear it!" And he turned on his heels and walked back inside.

Maudie stood looking after him. He was certainly strange, all right. But she didn't have long to think about it because there came Anne Hubbell running right toward her, and Anne was "it." Maudie shrieked and took off again.

By the time Father came out of the school building with Mother's basket, Maudie was hot and sweaty and had to be cooled down with a glass of lemonade. They walked over to the trees that divided the schoolyard from the pasture. Maudie sat on one corner of the old quilt that Mother spread on the grass and helped pass around the ham and biscuits. Claire's box had been auctioned off to a tall skinny boy called "Slats" Miller, and she and Slats were sitting against the fence. Slats had his knees bent and they came almost up to his chest. Claire was daintily holding a piece of chicken, and looking as though whatever Slats was saying to her was the most fascinating thing in the world. Maudie pressed her lips together to hide her smile.

Just as she took another bite of biscuit, Maudie saw Aunt Sylvie and Horace Benson sitting on a bench behind the school with Aunt Sylvie's box on Horace's lap. Maudie sprang to her feet and skipped over. There was an empty space on the bench between them, and Maudie squeezed right in, right there in the middle, hugging Aunt Sylvie's arm.

"Well . . . !" said Horace Benson.

"Did you hear my piece?" Maudie asked her aunt, knowing that of course Aunt Sylvie had.

Maudie in the Middle

"You did very, very well, Maudie," Aunt Sylvie told her, stroking her hair.

Maudie could hardly contain so much happiness. "Really?" she said, wondering how she could get Aunt Sylvie to say it still again.

"Very well indeed," said Horace.

Horace didn't count.

Maudie swung her feet back and forth under the bench. "Aren't you going to open it?" she asked Horace, pointing to Aunt Sylvie's beautiful box.

"We were just getting ready to enjoy our lunch," he told her, and cleared his throat.

"Well, you'll like it, because Aunt Sylvie made a chocolate cake," Maudie said, hoping that they would offer some of it to her. She took another bite of biscuit before she saw Mother, motioning with one finger. She jumped up and skipped back over.

"Maudie," Mother said. "Stay with us, dear." She had the same kind of smile on her face that she often shared with Aunt Sylvie.

"Why?" Maudie demanded. "I wanted to eat with . . ." And suddenly she realized just how silly she had been. "Aunt Sylvie and Horace *Benson*?" she croaked, turning to stare at them.

"She could do a lot worse," said Father. "Even though he *does* have a mouth fit for a baseball."

Maudie in the Middle

Maudie sat down on the quilt again and looked around. Claire and Slats Miller, Miss Richardson and the choirmaster, Aunt Sylvie and Horace Benson. . . . She squirmed when she thought of the way she had sat right down between them! But by the time she drank the rest of her lemonade, she decided it didn't really matter. She was feeling too good about herself to let a little thing like that get in the way. It was easy to be good and love everyone when you felt that everyone loved you, Maudie thought. Maybe *real* goodness was being kind to people even when they weren't noticing you at all. Now *that* was hard.

When she had finished eating, Maudie went about the school yard picking up pieces of ribbon and silk and roses and feathers from all the boxes. She sat on one of the old rope swings, fashioning her treasures into a long chain to wear about her neck. When she got home, she would put it around Lucky, the new foal.

"This was a wonderful, wonderful day," she murmured as they rode home later in the wagon.

"*Wasn't* it, though?" said Mother.

Father only smiled. "You just wait until Monday," he said.

"What's Monday?" Mother asked him.

At that moment the chug of an automobile

sounded on the road in front of them. Joe leaped off the wagon and grabbed the horses' bridles as they reared up and neighed, their eyes huge. Mother held on to her hat as the wagon tipped and jiggled, and with much laughter and tooting of the horn, two young men from the box social steered their automobile around the frightened horses and rode on.

"Honestly!" Mother said, when the wagon finally started forward. She turned to look at Father. "What's Monday?" she asked again.

Father was still smiling. "You'll see," he said.

7

The Big Surprise

If only Maudie had been able to keep the good feelings going.

It wasn't that she didn't try. She was kind to everyone in her family that night. After she put the necklace of ribbons and flowers around Lucky's neck, she did her Saturday chores, helped get Violet ready for bed, took out a hem in one of her mother's dresses, and read a story to Sammy from an old school primer. She didn't even fight with Lester over the last remaining piece of Aunt Sylvie's chocolate cake.

Everyone treated her, in turn, like a princess— the girl who had recited her poem without a single mistake. When Maudie went to bed, she was already thinking about what she would recite for next year's box social. She hoped she could find something that was *really* sad, for she loved making her lips quiver. She would ask Aunt Sylvie the next day if she knew any poems that would make you cry. And she wondered how many more years it would be before *she* made a box lunch to take to the social instead of sitting on a blanket with her family. She imagined giggling about it in the kitchen with Aunt Sylvie as they worked on it together.

"Was he nice?" she asked Claire, who had just crawled in beside her.

Claire tugged at the sheet and pulled it up to her chin. "Who?"

"Slats Miller."

"If you are referring to Russell Benjamin Miller, he was a charming dinner companion," said Claire. "And for your information, *nobody* in his own family calls him Slats."

Maudie rolled over and didn't ask anything more. All she had to do was look cross-eyed at Claire, it seemed, and her sister complained.

By the time Monday came and the Simms children were on their way to school, Maudie had lost that special feeling she'd had at the box social. Vernon and Lester were teasing, for one thing. While Claire walked resolutely on ahead as though she belonged to some other family, Vernon and Lester were playing at being blind, and trying to see how long they could walk in a straight line without falling down into the ditch. Maudie didn't think it was funny at all, and was especially annoyed at the way they kept bumping into her.

"Stop it!" she said, and once, when Vernon fell against her with his lunch bucket, scratching her arm, she yelped and hit him.

"There, little girl, don't cry!" Vernon mimicked, and Lester immediately took it up.

"They have broken your heart, I know!" he wailed, wiping his eyes on his sleeve, and both boys doubled over, howling with laughter.

If Maudie had any glimmer of the good feeling left at all, it was certainly gone by now. She had been hoping that when she walked into the classroom Miss Richardson might say something special to her about her recitation at the box social, or perhaps some of the other children would tell her just how marvelous she had been. She was furious that Vernon and Lester would try to make her appear just plain silly. She swung at Vernon with her own syrup pail, only making him hoot and holler all the louder.

The day did not go well. Miss Richardson told

everyone how wonderful the program had been, but she didn't say anything special to Maudie. And when Maudie and Anne Hubbell were sent to a neighbor's house for water to fill the drinking pail, Anne slipped, and the water sloshed over onto Maudie's stocking, running down into her shoe and squishing with each step.

Maudie was still trying hard to be good when she got home that afternoon, even though she didn't much feel like it. She changed into her work clothes and began her chores. She sprinkled some clothes for Mama to iron, brought in corncobs for the stove, and drew water from the well for drinking. Then she pumped water from the cistern on the back porch to fill the stove reservoir, so that Mother would have hot water handy when she needed it. Mother had told her once that when *she* was a little girl, her family did not have a reservoir—that small tank on one side of the stove that kept water hot as long as the stove was hot.

"What did you do when you wanted hot water?" Maudie had asked, wondering.

"We had to heat it in pans on the stove," Mother said.

How dreadful, Maudie thought. Of course you heated water on the stove when you wanted to wash clothes or take a bath, but imagine having to wait while water heated just to wash your face! How much easier it was to dip up some hot water from the stove reservoir—there whenever you wanted it. Life certainly was easier for her than it had been for Mama.

"Where's Pa?" she asked as she brought in the second bucket.

"He and Joe went to Ireton, but he wouldn't say why," Mother told her. "It's all very mysterious."

That helped perk up the day a little. While Maudie gathered eggs from the hen house, she tried to guess what the surprise would be. Last summer it had been the Shetland pony and a cart. The summer before that it was season tickets for them all to Chautauqua, a traveling program performed in a tent. Maybe Father was buying tickets again this year. Maudie hoped there would be more trained animal acts and fewer of the speeches her parents liked to hear. Then she frowned. Father wouldn't have taken Joe with him just to buy tickets, and anyway, it wasn't even summer yet. No, the surprise was something else. Making a tour of the barn to see if any eggs were in there, Maudie found a hen in the hayloft sitting on more than a dozen eggs. Maudie decided to leave her be, and had just taken

The Big Surprise

71

the egg basket into the house when she heard a peculiar sound.

The boys had already rushed to the window. Maudie stared at her mother, Mother was staring at Aunt Sylvie, and even before Maudie went to the door and looked, she knew that her father had bought an automobile.

It was a green 1908 Oakland, with a front seat, a back seat, and a hood that could be pulled up over the top in case of rain. Maudie stood out on the grass staring as the others swarmed around it. Father, however, kept looking over at Mother, smiling shyly.

"Is it ours?" Mother said finally, walking slowly toward it.

"It's ours," said Father. "I bought it from Clyde Worthington. Almost new. He got it two months ago and was selling it cheap."

"But *why?*" Mother asked.

"Because Clyde's a brickhead when it comes to machines, Ella," Father told her. "Has no patience with them at all. Joe and I will keep it going." Father reached out to wipe a smudge off one of the headlights, then stepped back to admire it again. "Isn't she something!"

Down at the end of the lane, Joe turned in with

the buggy. It came clattering up the drive, and Joe grinned widely.

"Well, Mother," he said, climbing down and hitching the horse. "What do you think? Isn't that some machine!"

"I think I've got to have a ride in it before I make up my mind," said Mother.

Everyone piled in. Maudie had never remembered the family doing anything quite so spontaneously, forgetting supper, forgetting the cows that had to be milked. Mother sat in front between Father and Joe. Lester sat on Joe's lap and Violet sat on Mother's. In the back seat, Maudie sat on Aunt Sylvie's lap, Sammy sat on Claire's, and Vernon sat squeezed in between them.

"Are you sure it can carry all of us?" Mother asked.

"This is an *automobile*, Ella, not a horse!" Father said. "Got all the horsepower I need right there in that engine." And then, as if to make the excursion more festive, Father took a sack of horehound candy from his jacket pocket and passed it around.

The first order of business was to turn the automobile about so that it was facing back down the lane again instead of aiming at the barn.

Maudie sucked on the candy, and everyone

cheered as the automobile sputtered, chugged, bolted, backed, and finally turned itself around and began moving bumpily down the lane. They had no sooner reached the road, however, than they saw old Mr. Watts heading toward them in his Buick.

"Well! Tom!" Mr. Watts yelled, coming to a stop. "You've got yourself a machine!"

"Got it from Clyde Worthington!" Father yelled back, edging the Oakland forward just a little, and Maudie fidgeted impatiently on Aunt Sylvie's lap as the two men held their conversation. She wished she had taken two pieces of candy the first time around because, when the sack came back again, there were only a few sugar crumbs in the bottom of it.

"Well, let's see what she'll do!" Mr. Watts called cheerfully, and then, laughing, he charged ahead in his Buick. Instantly huge clouds of dust came swirling back on Mother and Father in the front seat.

"Tom!" Mother shrieked. "The dust!" She put her hands in front of her face. Maudie could feel the grit on her teeth already.

"Dang the man!" Father muttered, glowering, and dropped back even further, but he slowed down a little too much and the engine died.

Maudie in the Middle

"Should've gone ahead of him, Dad," Vernon chirped.

"You would prefer a wreck, I assume," Father said irritably as he and Joe worked to restart it. "You don't move forward, Vernon, when there's a blasted Buick in your path." With a jolt, the Oakland was moving again, and Maudie settled back on Aunt Sylvie's lap to enjoy the ride.

Joe was obviously trying to help his father out. "It's a great car," he said. "Mr. Worthington was crazy to sell it. Rode like a charm back from Ireton, Mother. Dad only had one blowout, and by the time I caught up with him in the buggy, he about had it fixed."

Maudie could tell by the way Father moved his jaw that he wished Joe had not mentioned that.

"You've already had a blowout?" Mother asked, warily.

"We have everything we need to fix the tires right here, Ella," Father told her. "Don't worry."

It might have been fun if they had driven all the way into Ireton and back, Maudie decided, but every time Father met someone on the road, he had to stop and let him admire the automobile, tell him where he got it. When the talk ended and Maudie thought that finally the real ride was about

The Big Surprise

75

to begin, Father would see someone else he knew. Then he would toot the horn some more, wave, and the car would wobble over, the engine spitting and chugging, as Father tried to keep it going without moving forward. If it weren't for all the stopping and starting, they could have gone to Hawarden and back by now, Maudie guessed.

Aunt Sylvie's knees were beginning to feel bony, and Maudie shifted her weight from one hip to the other. She wasn't even sure she liked having an automobile in the family. How would she feel at school, for example, when it was snowing, and she looked out to see her father sitting there, waiting for them in the Oakland? No horse blankets to crawl under, no straw, no lying on her back with her eyes on the sky, feeling the snowflakes land on her eyelids. The automobile was like having still another baby in the family, and Maudie thought of the days and weeks ahead when all Father and the boys would want to talk about at the supper table was the Oakland.

What happened next was not because Maudie was trying to be bad. Not that at all. It happened because Maudie just didn't think. She was growing very tired of the automobile. She squirmed on Aunt Sylvie's lap, licked the candy sugar off her fingers, unbuttoned the top button of each shoe, rested her head on the back of the front seat, and finally, just as the Oakland went over a gentle rise in the road and started down the other side, Maudie blew up the empty candy sack and hit it hard with the palm of her hand.

BAM!

Aunt Sylvie, who had been dozing, jumped, grasping at the side of the automobile. Mother shrieked as the Oakland swerved. Father, gripping the wheel hard, steered it off to one side. Joe leaped out.

"What is it?" yelled Father. "Which tire, Joe?"

Maudie froze.

"I don't know," Joe hollered back. "They look all right to me."

"It was *Maudie!*" yelled Vernon.

Everyone in the front seat turned around. Everyone in the back seat stared at Maudie. Maudie tried to melt away, to hide herself in the ruffles of Aunt Sylvie's blouse, but now Aunt Sylvie had her arms folded across her chest and her elbows were sharp against Maudie's back. *Why* had she done such an awful thing? Why did she never think?

Father was furious.

"Always got to start something, don't you, Maudie?" he roared. "Always got to have an audience. I've a good mind to make you get out and walk the rest of the way home. Almost made me run off the road there, thinking it was a tire, and it would have been you to take the blame."

The engine died once more, and while everyone glared at Maudie, Father got it going still again. The automobile lurched and headed home at last, everyone covered with dust, Father grim and angry behind the wheel.

Maudie almost wished he *had* made her get out and walk—wished there was some way that walking could erase what she had done.

The terrible thing about Maudie Mae was that she was like a lightning rod, she decided. She just had to attract trouble.

8

Feet

What she needed, Maudie decided, was forgiveness.
To turn herself into a whole new person. To be
as thoughtful and good as the pastor's wife, Sister
Bliss. Aunt Sylvie would never want her for a godchild if she continued to behave so badly. There
was to be a foot-washing ceremony at the church
in June, and Maudie made up her mind that this
year she would take part. Mother had already said
that she could. And so, with the promise of salvation
just around the corner, Maudie put her mind to
summer.

At school, Miss Richardson began reading still another mystery to the class, *The Castle of Otranto,* capturing by force the eighth-grade boys whose bodies were larger and voices louder than Miss Richardson's. Sometimes even a story wouldn't hold them, however, and on those days, when the squeaks of the desks and benches grew loudest, she would simply put down what she was reading and say, "Songbooks, please!" It didn't matter that they had had music only that morning; they would have it again in the afternoon, and, with Claire at the piano, they would sing away the fidgets.

The songbook was *American School Songs,* with a picture of two flags and an eagle on the front. Maudie's favorite song was "The Cuckoo Clock," and her least favorite was a stupid one called "Boys May Whistle, Girls Must Sing." Anne Hubbell always requested that song, and Maudie could never understand why. Every boy in the room, however, seemed to like a song called "Jolly Boys," because the chorus went, "Slap, bang, here they come again, what jolly boys are they. . . ." And at the "slap" and the "bang," everyone could pound his desk. Lester always took out his geography book, which was largest of all his books, and banged it down as hard as he could.

At recess Miss Richardson came out in the yard

with them. They chose up sides, and half the children went to the front of the school, while the other half stayed in back. The teacher would stand where she could see both sides. Then someone would call "Ante-over" and throw the ball over the roof of the school. If the other side caught the ball, the catcher would race around the building and try to tag as many children as possible. Those who were caught had to go over to the other side. The excitement was almost too much for Maudie, wondering from which side of the building the runner would come, and which way she should go to escape.

On the last day of school, Maudie straightened the books on the library shelf—*Pollyana, Little Women, Rebecca of Sunnybrook Farm*—all the books the school official had brought from time to time in a basket, taking those that had been read to still another school in exchange. Maudie cleaned the blackboard, reluctant to let Miss Richardson go, afraid that she might not come back. Unsure of Aunt Sylvie, and with Mother so busy, it seemed important to Maudie that she be able to count on somebody. The teacher seemed to know what Maudie was feeling because she said, "I'm going to Cedar Rapids to stay with my sister for a few months, Maudie. I'll see you again in the fall."

Feet

Maudie went over to her teacher's desk, wanting to say something but not knowing exactly what. What she really wanted to do was hug her, but instead she reached for Miss Richardson's long watch chain and turned it around and around in her hand.

"I want to be a teacher," she said softly.

"Do you, Maudie?"

Maudie nodded.

"You'd need to pass the eighth-grade examination, you know, and go to high school."

"I know."

"I'm sure you could do it if you really wanted to," Miss Richardson told her.

It was like a bargain: Miss Richardson would come back in the fall, and Maudie, eventually, would become a teacher.

Vernon and Lester had already run home, whooping and throwing their caps in the air, and Slats Miller had come for Claire in his father's buggy, so Maudie walked home alone, the sun warm on her face. Halfway there, she realized that summer vacation had really come, and that she wouldn't have to put on her shoes again until September— except for church, of course. And suddenly Maudie was whooping and running too, racing down the road toward home.

Maudie in the Middle

The first week of vacation all she did, it seemed, was play. With Vernon, Lester, and Sammy, Maudie swung on ropes in the barn, from one pile of hay to another. They strung a rope from a high branch of an elm and tied a gunnysack filled with straw to the other end. Holding the gunnysack, they would climb up on a branch of a neighboring tree, jump off, and go sailing out over the ground below, straddling the gunnysack. They even made a little chair swing for Violet out in the grove.

Joe made a merry-go-round for them too, by pounding a post in the ground and loosely attaching a board on top of it with a bolt. While bees buzzed around Father's hive at the back of the garden and clouds changed pattern overhead, Maudie would sit at one end of the plank, Lester would sit at the other, and they would push their feet against the ground and go around and around by the hour, almost, until Aunt Sylvie declared it made her dizzy just to watch.

Sometimes Maudie played by herself in the grove, tying twine from tree to tree, making rooms for her "house" and using old boxes and orange crates for the furniture. Sammy would be her child for the day, and she would let him make mud cakes on an old piece of stove they had found. On days when it rained, she and Lester and Sammy wrapped

Feet

themselves in blankets and rolled down the stairs, landing with a thud at the bottom. Or else they would play church, using the stairs as pews.

The first two weeks of vacation went by so fast, in fact, that before Maudie knew it, it was the second Sunday in June, the time of the foot-washing ceremony at church, the time that Maudie had decided she could turn herself into a whole new person, her sins behind her.

"Be sure your petticoats are clean," Mother told both girls, and Maudie thought how embarrassing it would be if Sister Bliss chose to wash Maudie's feet and saw a graying petticoat sticking out from beneath her dress.

That evening some of the family took the two-seater surrey; the others went in the Oakland. They had to leave the Oakland out on the side of the road because there was such a large crowd for the foot-washing. Inside, the choir was taking its place in front. Maudie could see the white tablecloths that covered the bread and grape juice to be used for the Lord's Supper and the large ceramic basins for the foot-washing. It was all very mysterious.

Brother Bliss was a tall, thin man who looked as though he had been stretched. His forehead was unusually long, and there was some distance between his nose and upper lip. *Jack Spratt, could eat no fat* . . . The words came to Maudie's head before she could stop them. She frowned slightly to shut them out, concentrating hard on his opening prayer.

After that, everyone rose to sing "Rock of Ages," and then Brother Bliss read the Scripture. There were more hymns, including one by the choir, and this was followed by Brother Bliss remembering all the sick in prayer.

While the sick were being remembered, Maudie was thinking about feet—about how feet and summer seemed to go together. Just as she and her brothers took off their shoes on the first day of summer vacation, signaling a new season, taking off her shoes and stockings here in church for the foot washing meant the start of a new kind of life, perhaps, for her. After her own feet had been washed, she would humble herself by kneeling in front of someone else and washing another's feet, just as Jesus had done with his disciples.

She looked about her as the prayer went on. What a strange feeling to know that every woman there was wearing a clean petticoat and stockings tonight. The men would go to the back of the church to wash each other's feet while the women stayed in front, and when the foot washing was over and they had all come together again for the last hymn

Feet

85

and prayer, ankles would have been seen that were never seen at any other time of the year. Even the ankles of Sister Bliss! Maudie frowned and shook her head again, trying to clear it of silly things and think about goodness again.

The sick had been remembered and now Brother Bliss was talking about the Lord's Supper, or Communion, as the Presbyterians up the road called it. About being worthy in your heart. Old Mr. Watts, one of the church deacons, went to the front to help out. Then, eight or ten people at a time, the congregation went up to the platform to receive a sip of grape juice from a drinking glass and a little square of bread.

Violet and Sammy were too young, Mother said, to understand the meaning of it, but Maudie and Lester were allowed to go. *Gulp.* The bread cube was so small that Maudie ate it in one swallow. Up in the choir, Sister Bliss looked out on the congregation with her kind, gray eyes, smiling down at Maudie.

"This do in remembrance of me," said Brother Bliss, reading from Scripture.

When the family came back to their row, it wasn't long before Violet fell asleep, sprawled on Mother's lap, her thumb in her mouth, her round tummy moving up and down with every breath. Sammy sat leaning his head against Father's arm, his eyes closed. Every so often he opened his eyes halfway, stared at nothing, and closed them again.

Maudie leaned back against the pew and focused on a large moth that was circling around and around the kerosene lights. Her own eyelids felt a little heavy, and occasionally she opened her eyes wide and focused hard on Brother Bliss, who had now begun the sermon. But soon she felt them drooping again, and finally decided just to let them be. She could still listen with her eyes closed.

She was conscious after a while of her head tipping to one side and touching Lester's. She straightened up, but the next time she felt it tipping, she let it go. She was thinking about the little hole in her left stocking and hoping that it hadn't grown any bigger since she left home. But Sister Bliss wouldn't care. If it was the minister's wife, with her kind, gray eyes, who washed Maudie's feet, she would do it so gently, so lovingly, that a hole in the sock wouldn't matter.

Maudie heard music drifting in and out of her head, people moving about—then nothingness. Darkness and sleep. Music again. More darkness. After a time, Maudie felt as though the air in the room were changing. It had become cooler somehow, and there was a moist feel to it. Her arms

Feet

and legs felt heavy, her head much too large to hold up. Someone was carrying her, and the next thing she knew, she was in the back seat of the Oakland and they were almost home.

Suddenly her eyes opened wide. She could feel her cheek against Aunt Sylvie's shoulder. Sammy had his head in her lap. She struggled to sit up.

"What's happened?" she asked.

"You've been asleep," said Aunt Sylvie quietly.

"No, I mean, at church. What happened to the foot washing?"

"It's over, dear. You were sleeping so hard, we let you be."

"No!" Maudie bolted up, almost pushing Sammy off her lap. "I wanted to do it!" she bellowed. "I *wanted* to!"

"Don't yell, Maudie," Mother said from the front seat. "You can do it next time."

"Next time's next year!" Maudie wailed, her eyes brimming. And suddenly her words turned to sobs, and by the time the Oakland had pulled up to the house and shuddered to a stop, the front of Maudie's shirtwaist was damp with tears—angry, desperate tears. Her one chance to turn herself into a good person, the kind Aunt Sylvie might like as a god-child, was gone for still another year.

She was beyond control. While Violet looked at her sleepily from Father's arms and Mother herded

Sammy and Lester into the house, Maudie trailed after them, howling and flinging her arms about, hardly noticing where she was going. Joe, Vernon, and Claire had come home a little earlier in the surrey and were sitting at the table eating pie. They stared at her.

Maudie didn't care. She came crashing through the doorway, hurling herself against the woodbox. "You promised!" she shrieked at Mother in an agony of sobs. "I've w . . . waited all year. You p . . . *promised!*" She was blind with crying.

A hand touched her shoulder.

"Maudie," said Mother. "Sit down." Mother pulled out a chair from the table and gently guided her to it. Then she rolled up the sleeves of her dress, dipped up a pan of water from the stove reservoir, and poured it in a wash basin. Maudie wiped her eyes on her sleeve, her breath coming in little gasps.

"Take off your shoes and stockings," said Mother.

Maudie stared. Her sobs stopped in mid-breath. Mother herself knelt down on the floor while Maudie took off her shoes, then rolled down her stockings. Gently Mother put Maudie's feet in the basin and sloshed the water over them, then took them out one at a time and dried them on a towel. Claire, Vernon, and Joe had all stopped chewing.

When Mother finished, she silently changed

Feet

places with Maudie, took off her own shoes, and rolled down her stockings. The only sound in the kitchen was the tick of the clock as Maudie knelt on the floor, washing her mother's feet and drying them in her lap.

There was no music, no Scripture, but when Maudie was through, she marched off to bed, the family staring after her. It wasn't church, and it wasn't Sister Bliss with the kind, gray eyes, but it had been her own private foot washing. Forgiveness at last.

9

Hayrack Driver

There was a letter the next day for Aunt Sylvie. Maudie found it in the box at the end of the drive. The envelope was white and square with handwriting in black ink.

Aunt Sylvie was standing at the table, cutting strips of dough to put on the rhubarb pie. Maudie gave her the letter, helped herself to a peanut-butter cookie from the jar, and went into the other room to play with Violet. She loved getting down on her hands and knees to crawl after her baby sister, yelping and barking like a dog. Violet would shriek with delight and go crawling frantically off, in first one direction, then another. Sometimes, unable to stand the suspense, she would turn herself around and go crawling right into Maudie, wanting to get it over with.

Maudie chased her out into the kitchen, but suddenly stopped and sat back on her heels, for Aunt Sylvie's face was the color of the pink peonies that grew by the side of the house.

"Who's it from?" Maudie asked, as Violet crawled under the table.

"What?" asked Aunt Sylvie.

"The letter," Maudie said. "Who sent it?"

"Oh. A friend," Aunt Sylvie said, and tucked the letter in the neck of her dress.

"But *who?*" asked Maudie, because Aunt Sylvie had never kept secrets from her before. This time, however, Aunt Sylvie made no reply, and Maudie decided she'd better not ask a second time.

By suppertime, however, Mother knew, and she and Aunt Sylvie giggled together by the pump on the back porch. Finally, when Father sat down to eat, Mother mentioned ever so matter-of-factly that Aunt Sylvie had received a letter from Horace Benson, and by the following day, everyone in the family who could read had read it.

Maudie in the Middle

It was written on fancy white paper with a little picture of a tree in a meadow in the upper left corner. It said:

Miss Sylvie Thompson
Ireton, Iowa

Dear Friend:
I request the pleasure of your company in attending church this Sunday Eve. If I am correct in assuming that you enjoyed my companionship at the box social as much as I enjoyed yours, please do me the honor of a swift and favorable reply.

Yours sincerely,
Horace Benson

"Wonder what took him so long?" Father had said when he read it.

Now Maudie stood at her aunt's elbow as Aunt Sylvie answered his letter.

"Are you going to go?" Maudie asked, fascinated with all this letter writing when there was a telephone right there in the kitchen.

"He's a very nice man. I don't see why not," Aunt Sylvie told her.

When the envelope had been sealed and stamped, Maudie took it down to the mailbox at the end of

Hayrack Driver

the lane, delighted to have a part in this important business. She raised the little red flag on top so that the postman would know there was a letter waiting to be picked up.

On Sunday evening, when Horace Benson's buggy pulled up in front of the house, there was a Simms child at every window and two more out on the lawn, even though Mother had instructed them not to stare. Aunt Sylvie looked absolutely lovely in a blue cotton dress. She waited until Horace had come inside and talked a while with Father. Then she and Mr. Benson went out to the buggy and rode off together as stiff, Mother said, as iron pokers. Maudie could smell the scent of Aunt Sylvie's French perfume even after she had gone.

The summer days moved on lazily, and Maudie began to believe that the foot washing had helped. After the foot washing, there was Children's Day at church, and the pews had been decorated with flowers and streamers. All the children were expected to recite Bible verses at the service and to sing the new songs they had been learning all year. Maudie recited her verses perfectly, and carried the singing when some of the others forgot the words. Aunt Sylvie seemed to be giving her more hugs than usual, and Maudie was even getting along better with her brothers at home. As a reward,

Mother arranged for her to take piano lessons from Mr. Watts's sister, two miles down the road.

Every Thursday Maudie would set out barefoot, kicking the dust up behind her, her music book tucked beneath her arm. There, in the musty parlor, she would play her scales and exercises while the old lady tapped out the time with a pencil. Sometimes they would play duets—"The Dancing Song" and "Theme in G Major"—Maudie on the high keys, Miss Watts playing the low ones. When Maudie got home and played the songs on her own piano, she heard Mother say to Aunt Sylvie, "Isn't it nice to have another musician in the house?" "Indeed it is," said Sylvie. Maudie could have played all night after that compliment.

The goodness lasted on into July. Once she broke Violet's little chair swing out in the grove by trying to ride on it with her and they both went crashing to the ground. But no one was hurt and Joe fixed it again. Maudie repaid his kindness by taking him a glass of lemonade that afternoon when he was repairing the hoghouse, and she stayed with him until it was done, running to fetch things for him from the shed. She tended her little sister, distracting her with a toy when Violet begged for a cookie just before supper time, and seemed to spend half her life peeling potatoes for the evening meal.

Hayrack Driver

But by the third week of July, the heat of an Iowa summer began early in the morning before Maudie was even up, and it stuck to her all day. Mother would fill a washtub with cool water for Sammy to play in, and Maudie and Lester sometimes climbed in it, too. Other times they got in the horse trough with Vernon, Claire, and Joe. Then the water would fly as they splashed each other, and Maudie had to hold onto the side to keep from going under.

Summer was the busiest season on the farm. While Vernon and Joe worked out in the fields with Father, Claire and Maudie and Lester helped pick vegetables from the kitchen garden. It was all Mother and Aunt Sylvie could do to get the tomatoes canned each day and still have supper on the table by five-thirty. But there were still clothes to be washed, rugs to be beaten, and floors to be swept, and Maudie helped as much as she could. She found that by setting her mind to it, she could hold onto goodness a lot longer than she had imagined.

One week she spent an entire morning helping her mother wash clothes, while Claire and Aunt Sylvie stayed in the kitchen putting up green beans. The washtubs were set up in the yard, surrounded by heaps of dirty clothes—white clothes here, dark clothes there, and two or three other piles of assorted colors in between. Adding to the heat of a July day, the steam of the hot water shimmered up from the tubs, carrying with it the strong scent of homemade soap.

Mother scrubbed the knees of Joe's overalls on the washboard, her shoulders hunched, arms moving up and down, and then, when she dropped the overalls at last in the rinse water, Maudie stirred them around with a stick. While Mother turned the handle of the wringer, feeding the garments through one by one, Maudie stood on the other side and made sure they dropped into the clothes basket. Then, when the basket was full, they hung them up together, Maudie bending down to lift something from the basket, Mother pinning it on the line. When the line was full, they spread clothes out along the fence, draped them over bushes, and spread them out on the grass. How wonderful it was to go to sleep at night on sheets and pillowcases that smelled of earth and grass.

That same afternoon, after Maudie had worked all morning on the wash, she saw her mother heading for the peach tree, carrying a basket.

"Need some help, Mama?" she called.

Mother turned and looked at her. "You've already helped with the wash, Maudie. . . ."

Hayrack Driver

97

"That's all right," Maudie said, and they went to the tree. Maudie climbed up on the branches and picked the ones Mother pointed out to her.

"A little to the right, Maudie. No, just above your head. . . . Yes, that's the one," Mother would say, and Maudie would brace herself against the trunk, pick the peach, and gently pass it down.

As they walked back to the house later, Mother, carrying the heavy peach basket in one arm, suddenly reached out with the other and gave Maudie a little hug. They took a few steps together, bumping into each other, then Mother dropped her arm and they went on to the house. Mother didn't say a word—she almost seemed too hot and weary to talk—but that hug stayed with Maudie the rest of the evening. Something warm and wonderful seemed to swell inside her chest. It was goodness growing, beyond a doubt.

Haying time came all too soon, however, and it was this that brought a change for the worse in Maudie. The hay had been cut and left in the field to dry; now it was time to bring it in. Because Mother, Aunt Sylvie, and Claire were working all day in the kitchen canning beans and pickled beets, and because Vernon had been asked to help out at a neighbor's, it was Maudie who had to work with Father and Joe.

Maudie's job this year was to drive the team that pulled the haywagon or hayrack, as the men called it. She was good with horses, and even though Father helped her turn them at the end of each row, Maudie could keep the team going in a straight line, straddling a row. At first it seemed like a fun kind of job, standing there at the front of the hayrack, stepping higher and higher as more hay was loaded on. A machine called a hayloader was pulled along behind the hayrack and, driven by the turning of its own big wheels, it raked up the hay in the field, carried it to the top of the loader and onto the hayrack, where Father and Joe spread it around with pitchforks.

As the hours went by, however, Maudie discovered that it was no fun at all. As Father and Joe tossed the hay this way and that, the scratchy stuff blew into her hair and fell down the neck of her dress. Father and Joe could move around on the hayrack to keep upwind of the blowing hay, but Maudie was trapped where she was, holding the horses' reins. Her skin itched. Her eyes stung. Sweat rolled down her legs and back.

The only relief she got was when the hayrack was full and Father took over the reins for the trip to the barn. While the hay was unloaded, Maudie would sprawl out in the shade of the barn, but soon it was time to go back to the field again and the sizzling broil of the sun.

On the second day, Maudie was so tired and hot she didn't think she could bear it. At lunchtime, she longed to jump in the horse trough, clothes and all, but she would only be going back out in the field after she ate, to get dirty all over again.

Wearily, she walked over to the two-seater swing near the back door and sat down, waiting her turn at the pump. Sammy was sitting on a box eating a piece of corn bread. He wore only a pair of short pants, and he looked cool and happy.

"Your face is dirty," he said, laughing at her.

Maudie knew it should not have upset her. If she had the goodness of Sister Bliss, she would not have said what she did next. But all the time she was driving the horses that afternoon, Maudie had been thinking about how, if she were younger, like Sammy and Violet, she would have spent the afternoon playing in a tub of water. Even Lester had an easier job, herding the cows out to the side of the road to graze because grass in the pasture was scarce. He, too, could stay in the shade if he wanted. If she were older, like Claire, she would have been in the shade of the house, helping Mother and Aunt Sylvie in the kitchen. But because she was the middle child, she had been stuck out there in the sun.

"I'm glad *I* don't have to drive a hayrack," Sammy said, adding insult to injury.

Something sour seemed to rise up in Maudie's throat. "Well, *I'm* glad I'm not *you!*" she said. "You don't even belong in this family."

Sammy took another bite of bread. "I do *so!*" he said.

"No, you don't." Maudie leaned back in the swing and pushed on the ground with her feet. The chains made squeaking noises overhead whenever the swing came forward. "We're not your real family at all. You weren't even born to us."

Sammy stopped chewing. "Who was I born to?" he asked.

The story in Maudie's head grew wilder still, and she managed to look very sad. "I don't know. Nobody knows. But a long time ago, Mother heard a baby crying down by the road, and there you were, lying in the grass. She just took you in because she felt sorry for you. Somebody had thrown you away."

Sammy looked at her with his mouth half-open. Then he swallowed, laid his corn bread down on the grass, and before Maudie could stop him, rushed into the house, wailing at the top of his lungs.

Maudie waited, knowing what would happen. Aunt Sylvie came to the door and looked out. Suddenly Mother shot out of the door at a run, walked over to the swing, lifted Maudie up by one arm, and spanked her.

This was the girl who wanted to be a teacher? *This* was the girl who wanted to help small children grow? The goodness had gone again, taking Maudie's pride with it.

10

The Razor Strop

July became August, and threshing time was upon them. The wheat not only had to be cut, but its grains separated and then removed from the straw. This part was done in the threshing machine. The farmers helped each other. Maudie stood out on the grass holding onto Sammy and Violet as the big steam-powered engine, pulling the threshing machine, came puffing slowly up the lane, followed by the water wagon and then the neighborhood men with their hayracks.

Mother and Aunt Sylvie had been planning all week what they would feed the threshers, and they always asked, when Father and Joe came home from working somewhere else, just what the women had served. It was like a contest, Maudie thought, but without any prizes. This time Mother decided on chicken and dumplings, sliced tomatoes, lima beans, hot rolls, creamed corn, and peach cobbler.

All morning the hayracks, loaded with Father's wheat, came in from the fields in a steady line as the neighbors took their turns pitching their bundles into the feeder of the threshing machine. The water in the boiler made the steam that powered the engine. From where she was standing, Maudie could see the long belt that reached from the steam engine to the threshing machine. As the belt moved, powered by the engine, it turned a cylinder inside the machine, and the spikes on the cylinder knocked the grain from the straw.

Big puffs of smoke came from the steam engine when a new batch of coal was added to keep the water hot, and the threshing machine would spit out grain from one spout and straw from another in a huge pile—straw that would be used in the barn for the horses and cows later on. Maudie knew that as soon as the threshing was over and the men had gone home, she and Lester and Sammy would run to that straw pile and leap about, sliding and burrowing and jumping and rolling until Father told them to stop. For now, however, her job was to keep the young ones out of the way.

At noon a long bench was set out with basins and soap and towels, and the men washed the dust off themselves before they sat down at the table. Some talked as they ate, while others took big mouthfuls of food and hardly said a word. Maudie and Lester worried that there might not be any food left, but there were little dabs of this and that, and when Maudie finished eating at last, she was full.

The whole point of threshing, it seemed to Maudie, was the meal, and it would have been unthinkable if the peach cobbler had run out before she had any. There were no foods that the Simms children would not eat. Never in Maudie's life had she heard Claire or her brothers complain that they didn't like this or that. They were always hungry when they came to the table, and what was on their plates was always good.

During that last week of August, Maudie did more than her share of work. Up and down the cellar stairs she went, carrying jars of vegetables her mother and Aunt Sylvie had canned, lining them up on the shelves Father had built. She changed the large sticky sheets of flypaper that Mother laid out in the kitchen, and cleaned all the chimneys on the kerosene lamps. She dug potatoes and picked sweet corn for the evening meal. Because Father and Joe and Vernon worked late every day in the fields, it was Maudie who brought the cows in at night.

She stretched out in the hay watching, while Claire sat on a little three-legged stool to do the milking, grasping the cow's teats firmly in her hands and tugging downward with first one hand, then the other, directing the warm stream of milk into the bucket in spurts. Maudie sometimes got a poem going in her head in rhythm with the sound: "*Old* man *Tucker* was a *funny* old man; *washed* his *face* in a *fry*-ing pan. . . ." If a cat was lurking about, and there usually was at least one, Claire would direct a squirt or two right in the cat's face, making Maudie howl with laughter. The cat always came back for more.

Maudie didn't mind bringing the cows in, and Claire didn't seem to mind the milking, unless the cow switched her face with its tail. The job that they both hated was cleaning all the different parts of the cream separator out in the milk house afterward—so many disks and awkward pieces. Still, Maudie did her work without fussing.

But at the end of that week, there was a second whipping, and it seemed to Maudie on that day that goodness had left her forever and badness was multiplying like the numbers tables in her arithmetic book. On that particular Saturday, after Maudie had worked so hard, Mother announced that she, Aunt Sylvie, Father, Joe, and Claire were going to Hawarden for the day in the Oakland.

"*I* want to go!" Maudie protested. She had only been to Hawarden a couple of times in her life, and there was *so* much more to see there than there was in Ireton. Hawarden was still so new and wonderful to her, in fact, that last year when she was there, she and Lester thought they were supposed to take off their galoshes when they stepped inside a store, and the shopkeeper came over and said that it wasn't necessary. Maudie had been terribly embarrassed.

"*Please*, Mother!" she was saying now.

"Not this time, dear," Mother said. "Sylvie and I are going to see a dressmaker, and then we're going to talk to a milliner about lessons for Claire."

Maudie was frantic. "What *kind* of lessons?" she bellowed. It was sounding more mysterious and wonderful by the minute, and she was being left out.

"There's a woman in Hawarden who makes ladies' hats," Mother told her. "Claire wants to see if she might like to join the trade."

"I want to have lessons too!" Maudie bleated. She didn't care much about hats herself, but she'd do almost anything to get to Hawarden.

"You and Vernon need to be here to look after the others," Mother said.

"Why can't *Joe* stay?"

"Because the Oakland needs some repairs while we're there. We're going to have a man work on it while we do our errands and Joe wants to see how it's fixed. We'll be there most of the day, I'm afraid, but we'll bring back some caramels."

Maudie couldn't answer. All week she had worked extra hard. She had even washed the separator without complaint. Was this to be her reward?

She refused even to say good-bye when the Oakland left. She just sat out on the two-seater swing, her jaws clenched, pushing hard against the ground, and felt her anger rising inside of her. The oldest ones always got to go places and the youngest ones never had to do any work. It was always the ones in the middle who got the worst of everything.

Maudie in the Middle

Vernon and Lester were sulking, too, and each seemed to fuel the other's anger. All morning long they skirted closer and closer to the things they were not allowed to do. Vernon and Lester started it, actually, by letting the goat out into the yard and trying to ride it. Sammy squealed in merriment each time Vernon fell off. The calf was next, and almost got away from them. It was halfway down the lane before they headed it off and got it back in the barnyard.

At lunchtime, they ate nothing but pie—all the pie, gorging themselves past the point of comfort, just to make sure there was nothing left for the others. They chipped off pieces of the precious ice in the icebox and ate it—ice that Father and Joe had cut from the frozen creek in winter and kept under straw in a dugout back by the grove. Then, while Violet watched wide-eyed on the floor of the machine shed, they walked the narrow beams, with farm machinery beneath them. And when Violet had been put to bed at last for her nap, it was Maudie who got the next idea. A marvelous, awful idea.

"Blind man's bluff," she said.

Vernon made a face. "What's so wonderful about that?"

Maudie's eyes narrowed. "On the roof," she said.

The boys looked at her curiously. "*Which* roof?"

"The flat part just above the attic window," she told them. She wasn't even sure they could get up there.

"Boy, we'd really catch it," said Vernon.

"Mother won't know," said Maudie, and could hardly believe it was *her* voice saying such an awful thing. "Sammy can be our lookout."

"I don't want to play lookout," said Sammy.

"We'll *hear* them coming," Maudie declared. "You can hear that Oakland coming all the way down to the Wheelers." And then, when she realized the boys were ready to do it, she added cautiously, "There's only one rule: You've got to yell if a person's about to walk off the edge."

They took a dish towel with them to use as a blindfold and pushed open the small round attic window. Vernon wriggled out first, around to the steeply sloping roof at one side. He scrambled his way up to the top, then lay on his stomach, reaching out for Lester, pulling and tugging till he got his brother up beside him. Maudie was the last one to come. She tried not to look at the ground below, but let the boys pull her up, and finally all three of them were sitting on the flat roof on the very top of the house. So what if they couldn't go to Hawarden with the others? They could practically *see* Hawarden from way up here, Maudie thought.

"You're it," said Vernon and Lester, almost together.

So Maudie tied the dish towel around her face, leaving just a little slit below one eye so she could see a bit of the roof where she stepped.

There was a breeze up there that they hadn't felt in the yard, and the excitement of doing something they had never done before added even more of a thrill. *I don't care!* Maudie told herself every time she thought how upset Mother would be if she knew.

"Too close!" Lester yelled when Maudie got within a few feet of the edge, and she turned quickly in the direction of his voice, arms outstretched to catch him. Then she turned still again, swooping downward with her arms, and Lester was caught. There wasn't very much room on the roof. Down in the yard, Sammy sat on a rock glowering at them.

"You keep an eye on the road, now," Maudie told him.

Sammy shook his head.

Now it was Sammy in the middle, Maudie thought. He was too old to be taking a nap like Violet, too young to be up on the roof with them. Maybe no matter *when* you were born, you were

The Razor Strop

always too young for one thing and too old for something else. For the first time, she began to feel a wee bit guilty about being on the roof.

Lester was cautious when he was it; he moved too slowly, afraid he might fall off, and in order to keep the game going, Maudie and Vernon had to let themselves be tagged. It was scariest when Vernon was it, because he clowned around, even after they screamed, "Too close! Too close!" Maudie began yelling "Too close!" when he was within four feet of the edge, because he always seemed to go a step farther anyway. Once his foot almost slipped off the edge.

They heard Violet crying at last.

"She's waking up," said Maudie. "Come on. One more game and we'll quit."

Lester was it, but Vernon allowed himself to be caught again, and this time he seemed even more reckless than before. Maudie suspected that he could see a little beneath his blindfold, because he got right to the corner of the roof, then stood there balancing on one foot as though he were going to put the other off into thin air, his arms going like a windmill while the others shrieked.

Sammy, down in the yard, was screaming, too, and as Maudie tried to quiet him down, her eye suddenly caught the movement of a horse and buggy pulling into the yard.

Maudie in the Middle

"Vernon!" she whispered. "Someone's here!"

Vernon quit clowning and took a step backward. "What?"

"Someone's here . . . it's . . ." Maudie couldn't breathe. "It's Father!"

It wasn't Father's buggy, and it certainly wasn't the Oakland, but it was Father all right, with Mother beside him, and they were both stepping down onto the ground, staring up at the roof.

For a long moment no one said a word. The silence was broken only by Violet's mournful wail from inside.

"Maudie! Vernon!" Mother said finally, such disappointment in her voice that Maudie's knees almost buckled.

Father said nothing at all. After tying up the horse, he went inside the house and returned with the long leather strop that he used for sharpening his razor. "Get down," he said firmly.

There was simply no excuse they could think of. Vernon still had the blindfold dangling from one shoulder, and Mother and Father had seen him clowning around there at the edge. The flat roof was visible from halfway down the lane, and to Mother and Father, it must have been like watching a show on stage as they pulled up into the yard.

"Get down," Father ordered again.

Maudie felt sick. She shook her head and sat

The Razor Strop

down. Lester sat down beside her. Vernon peered over the edge of the roof at the ground and then glanced back at his father, standing there with the razor strop. He sat down as well.

"Take your time," said Father, and leaned against a tree.

Mother went into the house to tend to Violet.

"In case you're wondering," Father went on, "the repairman said that the automobile wouldn't be done until this evening sometime, and lent us his horse and buggy to come on home. Sylvie and Claire and Joe will stay in Hawarden till the Oakland's ready, and then I'll drive the buggy back. Anybody want to tell me what went on *here* this afternoon, other than what I can see with my own eyes?"

Nobody did.

"Who's coming down first?" Father asked.

Still no answer. Maudie remembered the whipping Joe once got for walking the rim of the silo before the roof was on. She remembered the trouble Vernon got into for crawling up on the roof of the barn, and the spanking Lester got for climbing the windmill. One part of her knew that she deserved a whipping and the other part was still angry that she had not been taken to Hawarden.

"Well," Father said at last, "I could throw some pillows up there if you want. Don't think there's to be any rain tonight to speak of."

Maudie in the Middle

Lester began to cry.

Maudie looked down at the sloping roof. It had been easier somehow being hoisted up than it would be getting back down again. Vernon began to mutter the same thing. The only possible way any of them could see to get down off the roof was to dangle off the edge by their arms, dropping down onto the roof of the front porch, and then dangling again for the drop to the ground.

They went one at a time, Vernon first. Father got up on the railing, and when Vernon lowered himself down to the porch roof and then dangled in turn from that, Father reached out a hand to steady him. When Vernon's feet reached the porch floor, however, Maudie could hear the *whack, whack, whack* of the razor strop against Vernon's overalls. Vernon never cried. Maudie only knew it was over when the whacking stopped and the screen door slammed.

Lester went next to get it over with. This time Maudie counted the number of whacks, wondering if Father would whip him less because he was younger. The same number exactly. Lester yelped.

And then it was Maudie's turn. She couldn't imagine how she had gotten up so high in the first place. She slid along to the edge, grit from the shingles sticking to the palms of her hands. Then, turning around, she held onto the edge of the high roof

The Razor Strop

and dangled a moment before dropping onto the porch roof. Swallowing, she crawled over to the edge and dangled again until she felt Father's big hand grasping her around one leg, and then he was helping her down onto the porch floor.

She leaned over the porch railing, lips pressed together, eyes shut. She was embarrassed, angry, and sorry, all at the same time. *Whack. Whack.* Surely Father would go lighter because she was a girl, because her clothes weren't as thick as the boys'. But she counted six whacks, sucking her breath in on each one, determined not to cry, and when the razor strop stopped at last, she bolted through the sitting room and up the stairs, her backside stinging.

It wasn't any use, she decided. The more she tried to be good, the worse she got. She hadn't asked her father yet about being Aunt Sylvie's godchild, and now she knew she would never ask it, because no one would want her. Certainly not Aunt Sylvie.

11

Being Bad

She began to hope again when school started and Miss Richardson returned. Maudie's teacher looked rested. Her face was rosy and she had a box of new books for the library shelf. Maudie was now the only member of the fourth grade, not the third. Everyone had moved over a row, Sammy had started first grade, and Claire had simply moved on. She was staying home now with Mother and Aunt Sylvie, making hats on the side table in the sitting room. If she showed promise, the woman in Hawarden had said, Claire could come and stay with her in January and help out in the shop.

At school, goodness seemed to come easy to Maudie. When she raised her hand, Miss Richardson noticed. When she had a question, Miss Richardson was ready to listen. Even when Maudie upset her inkwell, getting the black stuff all over her hands and books, Miss Richardson helped clean it up and didn't scold.

At home, however, if work in the fields was winding down, work in the kitchen was even more hectic, and Maudie's mother had less time for her now than she had before. In the early, hot days of September, something needed picking and canning every day. If not the peaches, then the apples; if not the apples, then the plums. Pears, tomatoes, blackberries, grapes, corn, squash . . . The list was endless. There were baskets of vegetables on the kitchen table waiting to be canned, boxes of them on the back porch, the steps. . . . A bushel of bruised apples in the cellar waited to be turned into applesauce, yet no one had the time to peel them. Some days the kitchen was so full of steam from all the canning that Mother put tables out in the yard and the family ate their evening meal under the trees.

Half the time it seemed to Maudie as though Mother and Aunt Sylvie didn't even know that she was about. And if they did take notice of her, they always asked her to do something—bring more jars up from the cellar, pump another bucket of water

. . . Maudie hated weekends, and looked forward to Monday.

The second Saturday in September was even hotter than the first. It was too hot to practice her exercises on the piano, too hot to play with Violet. As Maudie started to go outside, however, Mother said, "Don't go out there, Maudie. Your father's collecting honey from the hive."

"I just want to go as far as the lilac bush," Maudie told her.

"I said don't go out!" Mother replied irritably, pouring a pitcher of sugar into a big pan of boiling preserves on the stove. "We'll tell you when it's safe."

Maudie went back to the side door and watched her father through the screen. The hive was at the back of the garden. She couldn't see any bees, not a single one, and Father was almost through. It was so terribly hot in the house.

She looked over her shoulder. Mother and Aunt Sylvie and Claire had just lifted a basket of apples to the table and had started peeling them as fast as they could. Silently, Maudie lifted the latch on the screen door, edged it open, and slipped outside. She went over to the wonderful thick shade of the lilac and lay down on her back, staring up at the sky, letting the breeze blow over her.

She glanced toward the house once and saw

Mother looking at her, but Mother didn't call her in, so Maudie decided it must be all right. The honey was collected and the bees had settled down, and there was no reason in the world why she shouldn't keep cool, especially since it was she who would be tramping out into the hot pasture later to bring the cows in.

She heard the buzz just as she was ready to roll over on her stomach. Maudie bolted up. A bee was flying angrily about her head. In panic, Maudie took a swat. Before she could get to her feet, before she could even think, the bee attached itself to her hand and stung her on the thumb.

The burning, searing pain worked its way into her hand and spread to her wrist as well. Her thumb was swelling, throbbing. . . .

Maudie gave a cry and rushed to the house. The screen to the side door was locked again. Sobbing, she ran around the house and up on the back porch, but the screen to the kitchen was locked as well. Mother's face was grim.

"Go to the cellar, Maudie," she said.

"I'm stung!" Maudie wept.

"You weren't supposed to go out there. Go to the cellar."

Maudie could not believe it.

"Aunt Sylvie!" she pleaded, but her aunt turned her back and did not answer.

Maudie in the Middle

In anger and humiliation, Maudie walked across the porch to the cellar steps, went down and sat on a pile of burlap sacks, pulling the stinger from her thumb. She was convinced now beyond a doubt that she was the least-loved member of the family and had the cruelest mother in the world. And the cruelest aunt. Maybe she didn't care if Aunt Sylvie never asked her to be her godchild.

With tears running down her face, their salty taste on her lips, Maudie imagined her mother and Aunt Sylvie caught outside in a storm and how she would lock them out; Mother and Aunt Sylvie freezing to death in the snow and how she wouldn't let them in. She knew even as she thought it that all they had to do was to appear at the top of the steps with their arms outstretched and she would run at once to hug them. But they did not come, and Maudie spent the afternoon alone in the cellar.

She could not stay angry forever, though, and the third Saturday in September seemed destined to be better.

"Maudie," Mother told her, "Joe's driving to Ireton to pick up some things for me. Do you want to go along and drop off some baby clothes at Mrs. Franklin's? I have some winter caps and sweaters from last year that Violet has outgrown. Mrs. Franklin's baby can use them, I think."

Being Bad

Maudie didn't particularly want to stop by Mrs. Franklin's, but she liked going to Ireton—going *any* place, almost—so she took the box of baby clothes and climbed into the buggy with Joe. Her mother was trying to be kind to her, she knew, and sitting there in the buggy, actually *going* somewhere, Maudie almost began to feel loved again.

"Joe," she said suddenly, wondering if he would know. "How do you get to be a godchild?"

"A godchild?" Joe gave the reins a shake and the horse started off down the lane. "You have to have a godparent, that's how."

"Well, how do you get a godparent?"

"I think it happens when you're baptized as a baby," Joe told her.

Maudie's heart sank. Was it too late, then?

"But I'm not baptized! We don't get baptized till we're twelve!" she said.

"What's wrong?" Joe asked. "How come you want to be a godchild? Maybe only Presbyterians have godparents, I don't know."

Maudie couldn't answer. The horse clopped along the dirt road toward Mrs. Franklin's, and Maudie thought about Anne Hubbell and the new dress she wore on the first day of school—a gift, she had said, from her godmother; Anne Hubbell telling how her godmother had taken her to Hawarden one day over the summer and bought her little cakes and cold tea.

The horse turned in at the Franklins'.

"I'll wait outside," Joe said, pulling up under the box elder in the Franklins' yard. The Franklins' big dog came running over and Joe stepped down to rub his ears.

"Come in," Mrs. Franklin called. "I'm in the parlor feeding the baby."

Maudie walked in through the kitchen. The remains of lunch still sat on the table—a few plates, a cup, a knife, and three pieces of pumpkin pie on a plate in the center. Maudie's mouth watered as she walked past the pie. The first pumpkin pie of the season! She hadn't had much of a lunch. Maybe Mrs. Franklin would offer her a piece. Mother certainly would have. Mother offered lunch to anyone who came by, from the Raleigh-and-Watkins salesmen, who sold extracts, to the peddlers with their cases of jewelry, thread, and buttons.

Mrs. Franklin was sitting in a velvet chair by the window nursing her baby.

"Well, look what we have here!" she said when she saw Maudie. She took the box and opened it with one hand. "Now won't these be just right for my Eddie? And shirts, too! You thank your mother for me now, Maudie Mae."

"Yes, Ma'am," said Maudie, and waited. Under her dress, her stomach growled softly. She hoped that Mrs. Franklin had heard.

Mrs. Franklin looked at her and then at the baby. "Yes, indeed, he's getting bigger by the day. By the hour, even." She stood him up on her lap and jiggled him until he burped. The potato baby was twice as huge as he was when Maudie had seen him last. Maudie smiled and waited some more. She wondered what it was like to be the only child in the entire household—the very first baby to be born into a family.

"Well, I see your brother waiting out there for you. I guess you're eager to be on your way," Mrs. Franklin said at last. "Thank you for stopping by with the clothes."

"You're welcome," Maudie told her.

She turned slowly, trying to make her stomach rumble again, and walked toward the kitchen. Surely any moment Mrs. Franklin would say, "And take a piece of that pie with you." What did a man and woman need with *three* pieces of pie, when their baby hardly had any teeth?

By the time Maudie reached the doorway to the kitchen, she knew she was going to take a piece of that pie. Either Mrs. Franklin had simply forgotten to offer her some or she had no manners whatsoever. Maudie knew exactly which piece she would take, too—the large one on the end. Scarcely slowing her steps, she reached out with both hands, scooped up the piece, and was heading for the back door when Mr. Franklin opened the screen.

Maudie froze, her back to the wall, one hand behind her, holding the pie.

"Well, Maudie Simms, isn't it?" Mr. Franklin said smiling, and went over to the basin to wash. "I see Joe's driving the buggy today. Not having any more trouble with the Oakland, are you?"

"No, the automobile's working fine," Maudie said, edging closer to the door. The pie crust felt soggy in her hand.

Mr. Franklin dipped his hands in the water and splashed some on his face. "We'll see how that Oakland does when there's two feet of snow on the ground." He grinned, reaching for the towel. "That'll be the real test now, won't it?"

"I guess so," Maudie said and, holding one hand stiffly down by her side, slipped on outside and climbed in the buggy.

She had thought, when she took the pie, that she and Joe could share it on their way to town. But he would know, she realized now, that if Mrs. Franklin had meant for her to have it, she would have put it on a plate. In a box, at the very least.

Being Bad

———————————

125

In fact, if Mrs. Franklin had given it to her, she would have certainly sent out a piece for Joe as well.

The horse started forward and Maudie sat rigidly with one hand tucked down between the door and the seat, the pumpkin squishy on her fingers.

Halfway to Ireton, Joe said, "You know something? I'd swear I smell pumpkin pie."

Maudie's ears reddened. "Well, I sure wish I had some," she said, " 'cause I didn't have much lunch."

"Don't you smell it, Maudie?"

"Could be somebody's baking," she said, and Joe didn't ask again.

In town, Joe hitched up the horse and gave Maudie fifteen cents to buy some penny stamps at the post office. "You be back here in a half hour, Maudie," he said. "Don't make me come looking for you now." Then he went down to the general store to pick up the bolt of sailcloth and some bananas that Mother wanted.

As soon as he was out of sight, Maudie walked quickly down the sidewalk to the alley between the bank and the feed store. She held the fifteen cents in one hand and the pie in the other. It was beginning to ooze between her fingers.

It looked much too awful to eat. Maudie dropped it in a barrel behind the store, and wiped her hand on the grass. Then she went down to the horse trough at the end of the street and ran her hand through the water. She didn't want to see anyone. Hardly even wanted to go into the post office. When Joe came out at last, Maudie was already waiting for him by the buggy. The reward for being good wasn't much, she thought, but the reward for being bad wasn't any better.

She had a marvelous thought on her way home from Ireton, however. If Maudie wasn't baptized until she was twelve, maybe *that* was when Aunt Sylvie would ask her if she wanted to be her godchild.

Maudie would drop hints. She would ask her father's permission for Aunt Sylvie to be her godmother. If Aunt Sylvie said she would make Maudie her godchild when she was twelve, Maudie would never be bad again, not ever! She wouldn't fight with her brothers, tease Sammy, sass back, climb on the roof, listen in on the telephone line. She'd be perfect! She would promise!

That evening at dinner, Maudie thought her aunt looked different somehow. Was it her hair? Her cheeks? A new brooch on her shirtwaist, maybe? Something about her eyes? Had she had the same idea that Maudie did?

As soon as Father had asked the blessing, Mother said, "Tom, Sylvie's got an announcement."

Even *Mother* looked different, Maudie thought.

Being Bad

127

Both she and Aunt Sylvie were smiling that strange smile they had between them.

"An announcement, eh?" said Father, reaching for the boiled turnips. "Now *that* sounds mighty serious."

Aunt Sylvie didn't even lift her eyes from the tablecloth. "I have been asked," she said, "by a certain gentleman, to become Mrs. Horace Benson, and I said yes."

"Well, *Sylvie!*" said Father, and reached across the table to squeeze her arm.

"Now *that's* some news!" said Joe.

"Oh, Sylvie!" said Claire, smiling.

Maudie could only stare, not quite sure what it would mean. A wedding! Aunt Sylvie, a bride! Her head buzzed with excitement.

"Where are you going to live? Move in with his parents?" Father asked.

"No, no," said Sylvie. "Horace has bought a farm, Tom! It's in South Dakota, but it's where he wants to be."

South Dakota! A whole state away? Maudie put down her fork, her appetite gone. If she hadn't told Horace Benson what Aunt Sylvie's box looked like at the social, he might never have picked the right one. And if he hadn't eaten with Aunt Sylvie that day, he might never have invited her to church.

Maudie in the Middle

And if he hadn't invited her to church, she wouldn't be sitting here now talking about moving to another state.

It occurred to Maudie that all of the bad things she had done in the last six months had piled up one on top of the other until they had brought down a punishment worse than almost anything she could imagine. There would be no talk of a godchild now. Lovely Aunt Sylvie was going away.

12

Saying Good-bye

Maudie tried to undo it all in her mind. For days she could think of nothing else except meeting Horace Benson in the schoolyard and telling him about Aunt Sylvie's box. She imagined she had another chance. She imagined telling him that her aunt's box had green and yellow polka dots on it, or orange and brown stripes. Then he would discover that Maudie was lying, and would want nothing more to do with the Simms family ever again.

"Well, Maudie," her father said to her one night as they sat listening to Aunt Sylvie play the piano, and Maudie had whispered to him her awful secret. "If Horace hadn't sat with her *that* afternoon, he would have sat with her another. And if it wasn't Horace Benson asking her to marry him, it would be someone else. We all knew that Sylvie wouldn't be here forever."

They had? Not Maudie. *She* hadn't known it. She was miserable.

As if to match her mood, the hot spell vanished as suddenly as it had come. When September became October, Maudie woke to find the room cold, and when she walked to school with Vernon, Lester, and now Sammy, she knew they would soon have to get out the long underwear they all hated.

Mother removed all the old straw from their mattresses, washed and dried the mattress tickings, or covers, and filled them with clean straw. The only room in the house with a store-bought mattress was the guest room where Aunt Sylvie slept. The rest of the family dragged their huge newly-puffed mattresses back to their beds. The mattresses were so high and lumpy that they were difficult to sleep on without rolling off. Maudie and Lester loved to bounce around to flatten them out, and how the dust did fly!

Saying Good-bye

The days were growing shorter, a reminder to Maudie that their time left with Aunt Sylvie was growing short, too. Maudie's job was to fill the lamps with kerosene, and she found herself lighting them earlier and earlier in the evenings. The big iron stove in the kitchen was kept going all the time, and after supper Father lit the heater in the parlor. When the weather got really cold, they would close the sliding doors to the parlor to save heat and spend their time in the kitchen and the sitting room. But for now it was simply a matter of getting out all the winter underwear and sorting through it.

Vernon wore clothes that Joe had outgrown, Maudie took those too small for Claire, Lester got Vernon's castoffs, and Sammy got Lester's. At church one Sunday morning, Maudie found herself standing on the big heat register in the floor so she could feel the hot air warm her legs. She was trying to get as toasty as possible before Sister Bliss took all the children to the room in back where she would give them little cards with a colored Bible picture on it and a memory verse. They would practice saying the verse together, then one at a time, and Sister Bliss in her sweet gentle voice would tell them a Bible story.

There were cold days and warm. Clearly, winter was coming, yet there was still work to be done in the fields. Everyone, even Mother, helped husk corn to feed the livestock. One cold morning, Maudie's husking mittens were soon wet from the frost and her fingers numb. In hot weather, she often tried to remember what it felt like to be cold, but now, as she stood shivering in the frozen fields, she put her mind to summer. They *all* talked of summer while they worked—of what it felt like to be standing up on the hayrack. Then Mother got them thinking about some of the shows they had seen at Chautauqua.

Maudie's favorite was a performance of Pamihaski and his trained pets. But Mother's favorite was a comedy act where a woman came on stage wearing a lace curtain for a wedding veil, holding a vase of flowers, and singing, "My Wedding Day." When the song was over, she took the flowers out of the vase and drank the water. Maudie had never seen her mother laugh so hard at Chautauqua. Even now in the field, remembering, Mother laughed all over again. What Maudie was thinking about, however, was not the woman wearing the lace curtain, but how her own Aunt Sylvie would soon be a bride, and a lonely kind of sadness welled up in Maudie and stayed with her throughout the day.

She could not stand Horace Benson. He came regularly now to court Aunt Sylvie, always on Saturday evenings and usually Thursdays as well. Sometimes he brought his musical saw and his violin bow. Then he and Aunt Sylvie would play a song together, Aunt Sylvie at the piano. While the boys stared, Horace Benson would hold the wider end of the saw between his knees, and bend the other end way over. By bending the saw this way and that and running the bow over the edge of it, he could make as fine a tune as old Mr. Watts could make on a fiddle. But it was the only thing about him that Maudie liked. Sometimes he and Aunt Sylvie would sit together in the parlor or out on the porch, and Horace would put his arm around her shoulder. Every time Maudie or one of her brothers would look in that direction, Mother would say quietly, "Maudie, no," or "Lester, don't."

There were two good things that always happened at the end of October. One was Maudie's birthday on October 27, the same day as Theodore Roosevelt's. Last year, when Roosevelt was president, Maudie had written him a letter to tell him that they shared the same birth date, and back came a birthday card from the White House. Maudie had carried it around with her for several days, and Miss Richardson showed it to the others at school.

The other thing about October that Maudie liked, of course, was Halloween. Once, when their old dog Jeremiah was alive, it was so warm on Halloween that the family sat out on the porch after supper. Maudie got the notion to scare them, so she slipped into the house, took a bed sheet and, going out the side door, made her way through the weeds to the road. She wrapped the sheet around her and started the slow walk up the drive toward the house.

There were two things she hadn't counted on, however. First, that she couldn't see through the sheet, and second, Jeremiah. Maudie had gone halfway up the lane to the place where the lilac bushes stopped and the family could see her coming, when she heard the light thud of padded feet on the dirt and the pant of the dog. Then, before she knew it, Jeremiah was leaping up on her, barking happily, and Maudie went sprawling to the ground in a tangle of arms and legs and bed sheet, to the great amusement of her family.

This year Mother let each of the children carve a pumpkin, and they lined them up in front of the house with candles in them, hoping for company, but none came. Aunt Sylvie carved a jack-o'-lantern, too, the best one of all, but it only made the ache in Maudie's heart grow worse, knowing that the wedding was that weekend, and Aunt Sylvie would soon be leaving.

Saying Good-bye

The next day, when Maudie got home from school, she found Aunt Sylvie in the guest bedroom, getting her clothes ready for the wedding. She had ordered a $6.98 bridal underwear set from Sears, Roebuck—a nightgown, bloomers, petticoat, and corset cover—with Hamburg embroidery and Paris lace, and she let Maudie try them on.

"I don't want you to leave," Maudie wept, standing there on the rug in her aunt's lacy bloomers.

"Part of me doesn't want to go either," Aunt Sylvie told her. "But you know what, Maudie? We'll write letters to each other. Every week you'll find a letter from me in your mailbox."

"Promise?" It was not as good as having Aunt Sylvie here and it was not the same as being her godchild, but it was something special nonetheless.

"Promise," said Aunt Sylvie, and hugged her.

Brother Bliss, of course, performed the ceremony, and Great-Uncle Wilfred came from Orange City to attend. Aunt Sylvie wore a dress of lavender silk, with a tight-fitting bodice and a matching hat, and afterwards some of the ladies cried when they came up to kiss her. Maudie didn't know why *they* were crying, but she knew why she was crying herself. Maudie sobbed so hard, in fact, that she had to be consoled.

The only good thing about Horace Benson was that once the wedding was over and he and Aunt

Sylvie had gone to Sioux Falls for their honeymoon, he brought her back to the Simmses' house and left her there for a week while he took a team of horses and set out for South Dakota to do the fall plowing. He wanted to have the plowing done and the house ready before he sent for Sylvie, he said, and Maudie felt somewhat better after he left. She imagined him having an accident on the way and hitting his head on a rock; imagined the horses running wild and leaving him stranded. Then she realized how unhappy this would make her aunt, and was ashamed of her own thoughts.

There was one perfectly wonderful thing about Aunt Sylvie's getting married, however. Miss Richardson gave a party for her at the house where she was boarding, just ladies and girls invited, and Mother, Maudie, and Claire were on the list. Maudie spent a whole afternoon just laying out the clothes she would wear and taking a tuck out of her princess slip.

Claire was almost as excited as Maudie, and dressed with care in an embroidered dress so thin that you could see the pink and blue ribbons on her corset cover beneath. Maudie didn't wear a corset yet, so she couldn't wear a corset cover, but how she wished she had something pretty to show through her own dress.

Just before they left that evening, while Claire

was still combing her hair, Maudie found a colored picture from Sunday school of a shepherd sitting on a hillside overlooking Nazareth, with trees in bloom and sheep in the meadow below. Maudie unbuttoned the top of her dress and slipped the picture inside, just over her chest. Then she looked in the mirror. The shepherd was showing through the cloth, and looked as though he were sitting in the mist. Maudie was very proud of her idea.

It was the first time Maudie could remember going somewhere after dark with her mother—just women alone in the surrey. Mother took the reins and, with lanterns bobbing on either side of them, they went to the party, where Miss Richardson and Aunt Sylvie met them at the door.

There were paper streamers on the fireplace, paper wedding bells that fanned out like accordions hanging from the ceiling. Each woman or girl had brought a gift, something for Aunt Sylvie's new life in South Dakota. A table in one corner held plate after plate of little cakes and sandwiches—not at all the kind of food that threshers ate.

They played games to see who would be married next, and games to see how many children Aunt Sylvie would have. Miss Richardson was as giggly as a young girl when a game showed that she was the one to be married next.

Maudie in the Middle

"The choirmaster, I'll bet," Claire whispered to Maudie.

Halfway through the evening, Miss Richardson announced that everyone was to perform something special for the new Mrs. Benson—sing a song or recite a poem or something else of her own choosing.

That brought on such whispering and chattering and exclamations of "I can't!" Maudie and Claire went over to whisper with Mother. Maudie did not want to sing by herself, and Claire didn't want to play the piano unless Maudie would sing, so it was finally decided that Maudie and Claire would sing a song together with Mother at the piano.

When it came their turn to perform, Mother said to the audience, "This is a song especially for Sylvie, to wish her good luck in the kitchen."

That made the whole thing particularly funny, because the song was "Vive la Cookery Maid," about a young woman who goes to cooking school, but everything she makes turns out awful. Claire and Maudie used to sing it in the kitchen at night with Mother when they did the dishes. Aunt Sylvie, of course, knew it too, and started laughing as soon as the song began.

At first the other ladies listened politely, but when Maudie and Claire got to the line that said, "But the stuff she concocted a goat wouldn't eat," they began laughing out loud.

It was the first time Maudie had ever performed something funny in public. She was amazed that she could do it without laughing. In fact, the longer the song went on, the bolder she and Claire got, and on the second verse, they began to act out the words as well.

"She started on doughnuts that wouldn't cook through," the girls sang. "She toyed with the soup till they used it for glue. . . ." Claire pretended to be lifting a spoon up out of a dish and made a face. The women laughed even louder.

"They took her plum pudding to poison the rats, her griddle cakes might have been used for doormats, with her biscuits her brother disabled three cats. . . ."

Aunt Sylvie's shoulders were shaking with laughter.

On the third verse, about a pie that was as tough as sole leather and heavy as lead, Maudie pretended she was trying to pick up something much too heavy to carry.

"She put it away and retired to bed," the song went, and Claire put both hands up to her cheek like a pillow and closed her eyes.

"A burglar broke in . . ." Maudie tiptoed forward.

". . . and upon it he fed. . . ." She pretended to eat. "When they came the next morning, the burglar was dead. . . ." Here Maudie fell straight over toward her sister, Claire caught her just in time, and the whole room finished the chorus: "Vive la Cookery Maid!"

It was the hit of the evening. No other act had made Aunt Sylvie—or Miss Richardson—laugh quite so much.

Maudie was in heaven going home, snuggled in the back seat of the surrey beside Aunt Sylvie. She was an actress, a singer, a comedienne! She had got through the entire song without giggling once—without even smiling. She and Claire were so good at it, in fact, that even Mother had been laughing at the piano.

She wrapped her arms tightly about Aunt Sylvie, and her aunt hugged her in return. "Such good friends I have," said Aunt Sylvie. "This was one of the happiest nights of my life."

Mine, too, Maudie thought. It didn't even matter that when she took off her coat in the house later and looked in the mirror, she saw that the picture of the shepherd had slipped down inside her dress so that half of it was under her arm. Her cheeks reddened for a moment, but she hoped that when the other girls and women thought again of this

Saying Good-bye

141

night, they would remember the way Maudie had sung a song with her sister, not the Sunday school picture that was sinking out of sight beneath her waistband.

At the end of the second week in November, Horace called to say that the farm was ready. While Father loaded Aunt Sylvie's things in the Oakland, Maudie walked with her aunt around the farm, saying good-bye to all the things Sylvie loved—the vegetable garden, the milk house, the grove, the plum tree at the back of the meadow. . . .

They rode with her to the train station, and stood on the platform as she got on board. Maudie waved, but she couldn't see because of her tears. She heard the hiss of the engine, the chug of the wheels, the shriek of the whistle, but when she was able to see at last, the train was just a little speck moving off into the distance, and Mother was saying, "Well, let's go home."

13

On Their Own

It was when they were butchering hogs, a few days later, that the call came. Some of the neighbor men were helping Father butcher out in the barn, and after the carcasses had been scalded, cleaned, and cut into quarters, Maudie and Claire and Mother, back in the kitchen, put the meat through a grinder to make sausage. Mother had just washed the greasy fat off her hands a second time when the phone rang—one long, three shorts, and one long.

It was Mother who answered, and right away Maudie knew it was long distance, and it was serious. Maudie's heart stopped. Aunt Sylvie?

"Yes, this is Ella Simms . . . Yes, Operator . . . I *am* holding on . . . Yes . . ." And then, "Ernestine! What's wrong?"

All activity stopped in the kitchen. Father, who had just come in with another pan of fresh meat, set it softly on the counter, trying not to make a sound. Everyone hushed so that Mother could hear. Aunt Ernestine was married to Mother's brother, Ward, and was calling from some place even farther than South Dakota. Montana, Maudie remembered. How far away was that?

Now Mother had one hand against the side of her face. "No!" she kept saying. "Oh, no!" There was a very long time in which she said nothing at all, just blinked back tears. And then, finally, "Of course we'll come." She hung up the black receiver and looked directly across the room at Father. "It's Ward," she said. "I told Ernestine we'd come."

They left two days later, Mother and Father alone. Joe drove them to the station, where they would take the train first to South Dakota to pick up Aunt Sylvie, and then to Montana after that. Their Uncle Ward, Mother told them, was dying of tuberculosis.

It all happened so suddenly that Maudie didn't have time to feel much at first. The day before she left, Mother had spent the whole time cooking, her face sad and grim, instructing Claire how to warm the baked chicken and where in the icebox she'd find the soup. Brother and Sister Bliss had agreed to stop in occasionally to see that things were all right.

It was the first time the children had been left entirely alone. Sometimes Father went to Des Moines on business, or Mother visited relatives for a few days or a week, but there had always been Aunt Sylvie there to take charge. Now it was Joe and Claire. Violet did not seem to realize that Mother was gone until the second day. Then she cried and clung to Maudie.

As if to prove to themselves that they could do it, the Simms children all fell to their chores the moment they got up in the morning and again when they got home from school. Joe did the milking, and Vernon and Lester fed the animals. Claire and Maudie, with occasional help from Sammy, took care of everything inside the house. While Claire darned stockings, Maudie emptied the mouse traps; while Claire made soda biscuits, Maudie made Jello. By half past seven in the evenings, the dishes were done, the floor swept, and the cream separator washed.

"When are they coming home?" Sammy asked after the first few days.

On Their Own

"We're not sure," Claire told him.

"Before Thanksgiving?" Lester wanted to know.

"No," Claire said.

The next thought seemed to occur to all of them at once. If their parents wouldn't be back for Thanksgiving, could they count on them for Christmas? Even if they made it back by then, Maudie thought as she peeled potatoes, there wouldn't be time for Mother to make her usual presents. She always made new dresses for Claire and Maudie and new shirts for the boys.

To take their minds off Thanksgiving, however, they all made plans for Christmas, and Joe and Lester even went out in the woods to choose the tree.

Every few days, Sister Bliss came by in her buggy to make sure there was food on the table and clean underwear in the drawers. Each time she took home a few clothes to mend, and brought them back with buttons tight, the seams restitched. And every few days a card or a letter—once even a picture book—came in the mail from Mama. Sometimes there was a letter from Aunt Sylvie, addressed to Maudie herself. Whenever she found a spare minute, Maudie wrote a letter back.

Thanksgiving Day was spent at the Blisses', and dinner was preceded by a long prayer from the minister that had Sammy almost nodding away in his plate.

That night after they had returned home, it began to rain, and rained almost continually for the next several days. Maudie and Claire put on raincoats and slogged across the muddy clearing to put pails north of the barn to catch water, which they would use for washing their hair and their slips and dresses.

Everything in the house felt damp. Even the keys on the piano began to stick. When the rain stopped on Friday, cold took its place—a bone-chilling cold that brought even more mice into the house and sent Maudie rummaging about through the trunks searching out all the spare blankets.

"Brighten the corner where you are, brighten the corner where you are. . . ." Sister Bliss sang as she and Maudie and Claire washed clothes in the Simmses' milk house the first week of December. The milk house was a little building where Father kept the milk cans and the cream separator and, in a section at the back, the chicken incubator and corn cobs to use in the kitchen stove. Only the heat of the wash water kept Maudie warm at all. The walls blocked the wind, but even then her hands and cheeks felt raw, and when she hung the clothes on the line outside and brought them in later, the long underwear was frozen stiff, the arms and legs spread out like a person run over by a steam roller.

Mother called one evening. Maudie was boiling eggs in the kitchen so she was the one to answer the phone. Mother's voice sounded far away, over the swish and hiss of the long-distance line. Maudie had to shout to be heard, and Mother seemed to be shouting too.

"Is everyone all right there, Maudie?"

"We're all fine, Mama."

"Does Violet miss me?"

"She cried for a few days."

"What? I can't hear you, Maudie. . . ."

"She cried for a few days," Maudie shouted, "but I think she's over it now."

Everyone wanted to say a few words, but it was too expensive to talk long. Mother talked longest to Claire, and Father talked with Joe about the horses.

"When are they coming home?" Maudie asked as soon as Joe hung up.

"They're not sure," he told them. "Uncle Ward is failing fast. That's all Dad said."

Brother Bliss phoned over once and asked if they could take a peddler overnight. Joe had moved down to the guest bedroom now that Aunt Sylvie was gone, but Mother and Father's bed was empty, so there was nothing Claire could say but yes. They gave the peddler dinner and he gave them a box of salve that would have sold for a quarter and some ribbon. The next night he was back again wanting dinner, but this time Claire said no. There would be only leftovers to eat, she told him, but later she confided to Maudie that she didn't like the smell of the man's cigar. Father never allowed smoking in the house.

As a present to their parents, Maudie and Claire decided to embroider a pair of their sheets and pillowcases. Claire took one of Mother's best cambric muslins and traced a flower design on it from one of her shawls. Claire would embroider the edge of one sheet, they agreed, and Maudie could do the pillowcases.

Maudie's stitches weren't quite as small and even as Claire's, who had become quite a seamstress since she'd begun making hats. Each night, however, Maudie sat at the kitchen table with her sister after the dishes were done, sharing a kerosene lamp and making little blue forget-me-nots and pale yellow daisies on the edge of a pillowcase.

Time seemed to pass slower and slower as though the clocks were winding down, stretching out the minutes—the days—unbearably. Things that had gone right before now started going wrong. Claire and Maudie overslept one morning and then the stove wouldn't draw. It took forever, it seemed, to get the fire going just to make oatmeal, and then Sammy wouldn't eat it. Maudie and Lester tried to catch a rooster for dinner but couldn't, so they gave up and had to settle for fried mush with butter and syrup. Every day that passed without a postcard from Mama was a disappointment, but even when there was a letter in the box, it brightened things only a little.

The corn crib was getting low, and one Saturday they all put on coats and caps and husking mittens and went out in the field to husk more corn. Claire bundled Violet up with only her nose and eyes peering out, took her to the field with them, and sat her in a potato box. Though she ran all over the house now, in her heavy winter clothes she was so fat and swaddled she could scarcely move. They husked corn all morning till their fingers ached. The air was sharp and cold, but by afternoon they had enough corn for the cattle to last a week.

Maudie complained that her fingers hurt as she set the table that evening, and Claire snapped that she wasn't the only one whose fingers hurt. How would she feel if she had to spend the rest of the evening patching the boys' overalls? Claire wanted to know. The novelty of taking care of themselves had begun to wear off. As the days went on, Lester and Sammy seemed to be constantly at each other's throats. If they weren't arguing about who could play the talking machine, they quarreled over mittens or marbles or the last piece of raisin pie. Even Joe, at times, was snappish. Vernon had a stomachache, and to make it all worse, Sister Bliss had come down with a bad cold and couldn't come by for a while. Maudie and Claire had to wash the clothes themselves in the milk house, and it took them twice as long. They got them on the line only an hour before it turned dark, then brought them inside to finish drying on lines that they strung in the parlor, as Mother sometimes did.

Ten days before Christmas, Mother called again. Violet had been fussy all morning, and Maudie carried her into the other room so that Claire could hear what Mother was saying. When Claire hung up at last, Maudie returned to the kitchen.

"Uncle Ward died at ten o'clock last night," Claire told her. "They're burying him tomorrow."

After what seemed an appropriate silence, Maudie asked, "Then they're coming home?"

"Well," Claire said, "they're taking Aunt Ernestine back to Aunt Sylvie's to visit for a while. Mother thinks it might be a good thing for Ernestine, now that Uncle Ward is gone. She wanted to know if we'd mind if she and Dad stayed at Aunt Sylvie's for a few days, too. It would give them all a chance to visit together with Horace."

A few *more* days? Maudie thought.

"It's been so long since Mother and Aunt Ernestine had a good visit," Claire said. "They both want to see Sylvie's house. I couldn't say no. She said they'd be home three days before Christmas."

Three days before Christmas? They had already been gone a month! What was Mother thinking of? Maudie wondered. Didn't she care? Here they were, stumbling along by themselves as best they could, and she was going off now to visit Aunt Sylvie!

Even as she thought it, however, another Maudie seemed to be saying something else—another Maudie was reminding her of how few vacations Mother had really had in her life. Wasn't it time that she go, especially now that Aunt Ernestine needed one, too?

"We'll have the tree all set up for them," Joe said later when Claire told the rest of the family.

"And decorated," added Vernon.

To keep Lester and Sammy occupied, Maudie put them to work making Christmas decorations. She gave them a pan of small apples, pins to stick in them, old scraps of velvet, glue, and buttons . . . Violet, however, continued her fretting, and that evening, when Maudie was holding her in the rocker, she noticed how warm her sister's forehead was.

She stood up quickly and took Violet over to Claire. She could hardly force the words from her throat. Her mouth was dry.

"I think she's sick," Maudie said.

14

Holding Violet

It was the first time since Mother had left that Maudie saw fear in her sister's face. Claire rinsed out a cloth with cold water and laid it on Violet's forehead. They gave her sips of water, but the fretting went on.

When Maudie got home from school the next day, Claire was worn out with the task of caring for Violet and trying to cook for the family, too. Violet was crying hard now, and Maudie quickly changed into her old clothes and, holding her sister in her arms, walked her around and around the house. Again Violet's skin felt hot.

Maudie rocked her again after supper. Claire cut up an onion into sections and placed them about the room as she had seen Mother do when there was illness in the family, hoping the odor would kill the germs. But Violet was restless, turning and twisting and crying out, the heat from her body warming Maudie's legs.

Finally Maudie said the words she knew Claire was thinking: "Should we call Mother?"

Claire stood thinking: "They've left Aunt Ernestine's by now, and are probably on the train."

They called Sister Bliss instead, but her throat was too sore to even talk to them on the phone. Through her husband, however, she told them to take off Violet's clothes, lay her on a towel, and gently swab her whole body with cool wet washcloths.

Maudie drew a basin of water from the pump on the back porch and added a little hot water from the stove reservoir to warm it some.

They laid Violet down on a towel on the table and gently rubbed her arms and legs and body with the washcloth, first one side, then the other. Violet shivered at the feel of water on her skin, but grew more quiet, and afterward Maudie held her again,

Holding Violet

155

rocking and offering her more water to drink. By midnight, however, the crying had started again.

"If Violet's not better by tomorrow," said Claire, "we'll call the doctor."

It was the longest night Maudie could remember. Neither she nor Claire knew just how sick you had to be to call the doctor, but they knew Mother did not call him often. They took turns, one sitting with Violet while the other slept. Just when Maudie thought that the little girl was sleeping at last, Violet would squirm and cry, and then Maudie would hold and rock her some more.

"If she's not better by nine," Claire said, as the sky turned light, "I'll call."

By seven that morning, however, Violet finally went to sleep. Her forehead felt cooler. Her cheeks had lost some of their flush. Her nightgown and pillow were drenched in perspiration, but she slept hard, her lips open, her fingers twitching now and then. Maudie was more relieved than she let on. They should have called the doctor. They shouldn't have waited. What if . . . She couldn't even finish the thought.

In the days that followed, Violet clung to Maudie and would not let her out of her sight. Maudie stayed home from school, sending a note with Vernon to explain. Claire said she would handle the housework herself if Maudie would just keep Violet quiet. And so Maudie held her little sister, rocked her. Never in her life had she felt so needed. She was like a godmother, she decided, and Violet was her godchild. Hour after hour, Maudie sat in the rocker, Violet asleep on her lap. Maudie's legs would grow numb with Violet's weight. She could not read or sew or do much of anything at all, but still she sat there and rocked, and rubbed the little girl's back when she woke.

Since their parents left, Maudie and Claire had let Violet sleep between them in their bed upstairs, but now Maudie moved into her parents' bed at night, taking Violet with her so that Claire could get some rest.

The days, the nights, the hours, the minutes, all seemed to run together in Maudie's mind, a long succession of mornings blending into afternoons and afternoons into evenings. No one praised her, thanked her, even noticed her much. And when the letter finally came telling them just what train they should meet, it did not seem merely five weeks that her parents had been gone, but months, years, in which Maudie had grown and changed.

The Christmas tree was waiting in the parlor, decorated from top to bottom with the apple ornaments the boys had made. Claire had finished embroidering her sheet for Mother and Father, but Maudie had finished only one pillowcase. She wrapped them both to put beneath the tree, however, with a note promising to do the other one soon. Mother would understand.

On the day of their arrival, Claire and Maudie had the dishes done, a chicken cooked, the house cleaned, and Violet and Sammy dressed and ready. Joe, Vernon, and Lester had the cows milked, the hogs and chickens fed, and the cream separated. Joe had even taken his brothers to the barn and cut their hair. Now they all stood on the station platform, waiting for the first sight of the train.

"It's coming!" Sammy screamed at last, and they crowded closer as the ground began to shake.

Violet, however, was frightened by it, and as the train came in, belching smoke, its whistle shrieking, Maudie covered Violet's ears with her hands and ducked into the station. She waltzed her little sister around between the benches until the train outside had stopped and the passengers were getting off.

They saw Father first, waving at them from the door of the coach car, smiling broadly. He got down, then turned to help Mother, then reached up again for the bags and boxes the porter was handing down, some of them stuffed with Christmas packages.

But Mother's eyes were searching the crowd. Even before she saw them, Sammy rushed over and

hugged her legs, and Mother swooped down on
him, then Lester, hugging them both together. Vernon was next, then Claire and Joe.

"Where's Maudie?" Mother asked, her eyes still
searching. "Where's Violet?"

Holding Violet, Maudie hurried toward her
mother, who was rushing over. "Violet!"

Violet turned at the sound of her mother's voice,
stared at Mama and her outstretched arms, then
suddenly turned away, burying her face against
Maudie's shoulder, clinging tightly to Maudie's
neck.

Mother's arms dropped, her lips closed, the smile
gone, and suddenly she turned her face away and
cried.

Maudie swallowed. "It's Mama, Violet!" she kept
saying. "It's Mama!"

Violet clung all the tighter.

"She's been sick," Claire explained, coming over.
"Maudie looked after her for days and days, and
she's better now, but she just needs time. . . ."

Mother dabbed at her eyes, and this time she
was looking at Maudie.

"So you've taken my place," she said simply, but
her eyes were soft. Warm. Then her arms were
around Maudie, hugging her hard, even with Violet
between them.

Maudie leaned against her mother, loving the

feel of her hair, the smell of her skin, the sound of the taffeta sleeves rustling inside her cape. And then Mother said those words aloud that Maudie seemed to have been waiting for all her life. "Oh, Maudie, I missed you so!"

Joe brought the surrey around. Mother sat in the back seat with Claire on one side of her, Maudie on the other, and Violet on Maudie's lap. The others crowded in the best they could, squeezed in together with bags and baskets of presents.

"It's good you brought two horses," Father said, laughing. "We'd never make it home with one."

"With this snow, I didn't figure I should try the Oakland," Joe said. "Wanted to be sure we made it home without any stops."

As they rode along, Mother talked, then Father, then Mother again, telling about their trip—the sad parts, the happy parts, the parts they wished they could have shared with their children. Now and then Violet peeped out at Mother from the shoulder of Maudie's coat, then hid her face again, but by the time they were halfway home, Mother and Violet were playing a game of peek-a-boo, and both of them were laughing.

"She'll come around," Maudie said. "Once you're in the house, Mama, she'll remember. It will be just like it always was."

Maudie in the Middle

160

But it wouldn't be, not exactly. Because Maudie herself had changed. The way to goodness, she decided, was like the path to the plum tree. Sometimes you went straight ahead and sometimes you turned. Maudie might never be as blessed as Sister Bliss, but she might, some day, be as kind as Mother or Aunt Sylvie, and that was goodness enough.